# BLACKBIRDS

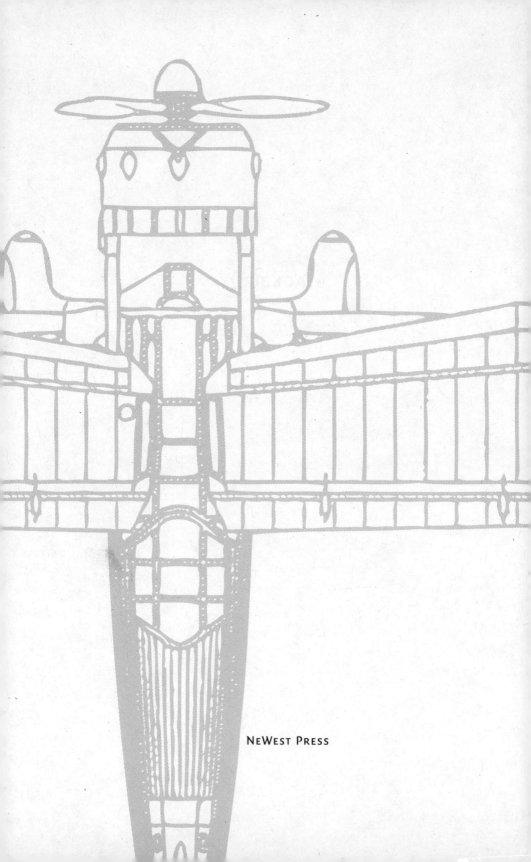

NeWest Press

Bill + Shirley,

Hope you
enjoy this one.

Garry.

A NOVEL

*Blackbirds*

# GARRY RYAN

# COPYRIGHT © GARRY RYAN 2012

LIBRARY AND ARCHIVES CANADA CATALOGUING IN PUBLICATION
Ryan, Garry, 1953–
Blackbirds / Garry Ryan.
ISBN 978-1-927063-21-7
I. Title.
PS8635.Y354B53 2012     C813'.6     C2012-902346-9

Editor for the Board: Jenna Butler
Cover and interior design: Natalie Olsen, Kisscut Design
Cover photography: (jet) micjan/Photocase
Author photo: Ben Ryan

 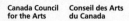  

NeWest Press acknowledges the financial support of the Alberta Multimedia Development Fund and the Edmonton Arts Council for our publishing program. We further acknowledge the financial support of the Government of Canada through the Canada Book Fund (CBF) for our publishing activities. We acknowledge the support of the Canada Council for the Arts which last year invested $24.3 million in writing and publishing throughout Canada.

#201, 8540–109 Street
Edmonton, Alberta T6G 1E6
780.432.9427
NeWEST PRESS    www.newestpress.com

No bison were harmed in the making of this book.
printed and bound in Canada   1 2 3 4 5 13 12

*for*
*Sharon*

The red-winged blackbird
of the Canadian
prairie is
unremarkable in
size and the female is
unremarkable in colour.
Little larger
than a sparrow, the more skilled flyers
of this species
will drive away intruders many
times their own size.
In fact,
blackbirds have been
known to perch between the
wings of an airborne hawk or crow,
and peck on the
head of the predator
until it
withdraws.

[ AUTHOR'S NOTE: Women of the Air Transport Auxiliary flew Spitfires later in World War II than is depicted in this novel. Also, Tempsford, or Gibraltar Farm, became operational later than depicted. ]

# CHAPTER 1
[ MAY 1940 ]

**"I already know who he is, and where he is."** Sharon Lacey watched the soldiers march past. They were like one entity, with arms and legs moving in unison. She heard the uniform applause of their heels as they struck the pavement. She saw their faces, the blank stares of defeat. Their helmets glistening with a layer of mist. *It's as if the whole world is wearing khaki,* she thought.

"Do you plan to do anything about it?" Linda Townsend crossed her legs and took a drag on her cigarette. Her red hair was cut scandalously short, and she wore a white flying suit with the front zipped down to reveal a white blouse and blue tie. She looked at Sharon, who sat next to her on the rock wall at the eastern edge of the airfield. The tarmac road running past the wall led to an army camp about five miles down the road.

"You think they're the boys from Dunkirk?" Sharon put her hands between the rock and a backside that was complaining about the rough edges of several stones.

"Their kit looks new," Linda said. "Their boots are new. Supposedly, they left the beaches with little more than the clothes on their backs. It's being called a victory. Our army plucked off the beach and saved from certain defeat by the Nazis. By the looks on their faces, they don't feel like victors." Linda looked over her shoulder. The fog was sifting away from the grass of the airfield. She could make out a low, red building with white window frames. "It's lifting." She carefully tapped the hot end of her cigarette against a stone, touched it with her fingertips, and put the remainder in the pocket of her flight suit. "Come on. If we get through today, we'll be off to White Waltham. It's a little airfield next to London where the ATA is beginning its operations."

"ATA? How come you British never speak English? It's all ATA, RAF, BBC, WC," Sharon said.

"Air Transport Auxiliary. We get to fly all the kites the big boys get to play with. The difference is, we're not supposed to have Jerry shooting at us."

*I'll never get used to this place,* Sharon thought. *Nobody speaks English. Jerry means German. RAF means Royal Air Force. Git means asshole. It's like learning a new language.*

An engine sputtered and caught.

Sharon swung around, using her arms to push herself away from the wall. She landed softly in the long grass. It swished against her flying boots as she walked. She looked down. The toes were already coated with dew. She zipped up her leather RAF Irvin sheepskin jacket as she walked against the wind. She watched the wings of a Tiger Moth shiver as its engine ticked over. The newly camouflaged green and grey biplane looked about as awkward on the ground as it did in the air. She turned to her friend. "Any news of Michael's whereabouts?" *Why are you so interested in her brother?*

Linda shook her head as she zipped up her flight suit. "Not a word. My mother is beginning to fear he's been captured by the Germans."

Sharon nodded. *We can't speak about the other possibility. The possibility that he won't be coming back.*

"Look at that." Linda pointed at the orange windsock whose tail began to flap as it turned into the wind with its open, fishlike mouth. "We'll get some flying in after all." Sharon picked up the pace. "Do you think Bloggs will let us do the cross-country today?" Sharon looked at a patch of blue sky to the east.

"Why not ask him?" Linda cocked her head to the left.

"You'd better do the asking," Sharon said.

"Maybe you're right. He found out you're a better pilot than he is." Linda turned to her friend. "A much better pilot than any of us. I'm afraid you've bruised Waverly Bloggs's fragile male ego."

"He's right over there." Sharon pointed.

Bloggs smoked a cigarette and leaned against the wall of the hangar.

Sharon said, "It looks like he's got his wind up."

Linda laughed. "You're beginning to sound like you were born here."

"My mother was always using expressions like that. I guess she never really left England." Sharon watched Bloggs as he dropped the cigarette and crushed it under the heel of his flying boot.

As they neared the hangar, the engine of the Tiger Moth sputtered and stopped.

Bloggs turned their way. He wore his freshly-pressed uniform jacket and pants. The final touch was slicked-back hair and a pencil-thin moustache. "About bloody time you two showed up!"

Linda reached inside the breast of her flight suit.

Bloggs watched her intently.

"We've got our flight plan ready for you, sir," Linda said. "Course plotted, winds estimated, and time computed, sir. All as you requested." She handed the plan to Bloggs.

Bloggs stared at Linda and then Sharon, searching for evidence of sarcasm.

Sharon raised her right hand to salute but was stopped by a glare from Linda.

"We're ready to go as long as the weather is accommodating. We were hoping you would have the weather report, sir." Sharon looked in the direction of the windsock.

"Met report, you mean?" Bloggs looked at the flight plan. "Headed for Ilkley. It's a longer than normal trip into ungodly West Yorkshire. Well then, get going, and don't get bloody lost along the way or you'll both be washed out!" He turned his back on the pair and walked into the hangar.

"We're off." Linda smiled at her friend.

Sharon leaned close. "Can't wait for some of that real home-cooked food from your mom's kitchen," she said.

"And a chance for you to walk over and introduce yourself to your grandmother." Linda headed toward the Tiger Moth.

"We'll see." Sharon followed with a knot growing in her stomach.

The knot grew tighter as they approached Ilkley. As agreed, Sharon had flown the first leg of the flight to the refueling at Digby, in the central part of England. Now Linda took the scenic route flying over-top of a castle Sharon's mother had often talked about. It looked much like every other castle Sharon had seen from the air on the way north. She was struck instead by the wealth of green. The fields that looked so tiny from the air. They were not as big as what she was used to back at home. In England, rock walls, rather than barbed wire, often fenced the fields. As Linda throttled back and lost altitude, Sharon realized the black-and-white photographs in her mother's album did not do justice to the spring colours spread out below them.

Linda added power to the Gipsy Major engine to clear a stand of trees at this end of a field. They settled onto the grass, bounced once, and rumbled over the uneven ground until they reached the end of the pasture. Linda opened the throttle and swung the tail around.

Linda shut the engine down. Sharon saw a grey-haired woman in a long-sleeved shirt and tweed trousers standing by a rock wall. She opened the gate and stepped into the fresh silence.

"Stupid British engineering," Sharon said as she tried to extricate herself from the cockpit without snagging her parachute, Irvin jacket, coveralls or flying boots.

Linda was smiling and placing the wooden wheel chocks on either side of the tires.

"I'll get the wings." Sharon pulled out two lengths of rope and a pair of pegs to tie the wings down in case the wind picked up.

"You Canadians and your rope," Linda said.

"Gets windy where I come from." Sharon undid her jacket and set it on the wing. The sun felt warm on her neck. She took off the flying helmet and combed her brown hair with her fingers.

"You picked a beautiful day for it," Linda's mother said.

Sharon stood and turned to face a woman with more grey than red in her hair. She was a stockier version of her daughter.

"Mom, this is Sharon. Sharon, this is Honeysuckle," Linda said.

"Remarkable," Honeysuckle said.

"Pardon?" Sharon felt the heat of attention from both women.

"The likeness is remarkable. It's like Leslie is back and no time has passed." Honeysuckle wiped at her eyes and turned. "Come on, lunch is almost ready."

Linda ran to catch up with her mother and put an arm around her shoulder. Honeysuckle hugged her daughter around the waist. "What's happened?" Linda asked.

Honeysuckle stopped. "No news on Michael's whereabouts."

"Oh," Linda said.

Sharon felt as if there were a hundred different places she should be other than here.

"He must have been taken prisoner." Linda let the sentence hang in the air like the promise of a storm.

Sharon followed along behind while looking over her shoulder for a possible escape route.

Honeysuckle glanced back. "Come along. We've got some catching up to do. There are stories to tell and stories to hear. Your mother and I were friends when we were young, that is until the old bastard put an end it."

"The old bastard?" Sharon asked.

"Your grandfather."

Sharon trailed them to the rear of a rambling two-storey farmhouse made of grey stone. The stone was stained darker where it had been weathered by water running off the roof. Vines grew up the south side. She got the feeling that the house had been grand at one time. That feeling was reinforced by the back garden. Colours she had never seen before ran rampant around the closely-trimmed grass where a table and four wrought-iron chairs sat on a flat expanse of stone with grass and moss growing in between the slates.

A woman with short grey hair, blue eyes, a grey wool skirt, and a sweater carried out a tray with a coffee pot and four cups. "You're here," she said, in a voice Sharon thought she'd heard before. Her stomach clenched and she shivered. *My grandmother! Cornelia!*

"Sharon, this is Cornelia." Linda rubbed her hands together when she saw the fresh eggs, bacon and toast on the table. "Mother, how did you manage this? Haven't you heard there's rationing?"

Cornelia held out her hand. It felt strong in Sharon's when she shook it. She pulled her hand away, while Cornelia seemed reluctant to release it.

The coffee, Sharon decided, was awful, but it had been so long since her last cup that she drank it anyway. She studied the garden while she felt Cornelia's eyes studying her.

"They've taken down all of the road signs. Apparently, it's to confuse the Germans," Cornelia said.

Sharon looked at the black-winged birds darting in and out of the trees. One swooped up, then down onto the tail of another.

Honeysuckle rested her cup on the arm of her chair. "Apparently, the invasion is imminent. The only thing stopping Hitler is the fact that he needs more boats to cross the Channel."

"Things are desperate. Everyone's got high hopes that Mr. Churchill can pull a rabbit out of his hat." Linda picked up a piece of bacon, put it in her mouth and closed her eyes. "Mother, where did you find bacon?"

"So desperate that women are going to be allowed to fly aircraft for the Royal Air Force." Sharon shook her head when she realized she'd added a thick layer of sarcasm to her tone of voice.

"It's the way of the world, dear." Cornelia patted Sharon's hand. "Men are always asking women to get them out of the messes they get themselves into. If Churchill hadn't sent the RAF into France in that lost cause, we wouldn't be so desperately short of pilots. Now he turns to you and Linda to get the job done."

"How do you know that?" Sharon decided that Cornelia was definitely becoming a nuisance. *That damned woman seems to want to touch me every chance she gets.*

"I told her," Honeysuckle said.

Linda smiled. "Father works for MI5."

Sharon frowned.

"He's in intelligence, dear." Cornelia patted Sharon's arm.

Sharon pulled away from the woman. "Keep your mitts off!"

Linda laughed.

"What's so funny?" Sharon asked.

Honeysuckle looked directly at Sharon. "She has a right."

"No. No, she doesn't." Sharon glared at Cornelia.

"She's family," Linda said.

Sharon looked out of the corner of her eye at Cornelia.

"I'm your grandmother."

"I know that, but I've just met you!" Sharon heard the sound of birds calling one another. *I'm staring at my hands.* She looked over at her grandmother's hands, searching for some similarity, some clue that they were related. The skin on the woman's hands was spotted with brown. There was a hint of dirt under the nails, something Sharon hadn't expected.

Cornelia took hold of Sharon's ponytail. "Your hair is the same auburn as Leslie's. It's the same silky hair, and you've got a cleft in your chin just like hers. I can see that you have her strength, too. You will need that, believe me."

"How long have you known I was in England?" Sharon asked.

"Almost since you got off the ship in Liverpool," Cornelia said. "Your blue eyes must be from your father."

"How do you think you got the new Irvin jacket and the sheepskin flying boots?" Honeysuckle nodded in Cornelia's direction. "She insisted on buying them and having Linda deliver them. She wanted you to be warm."

"Why did you never come and visit us in Canada?" Sharon asked.

Cornelia looked over the garden to a spot on the edge of the property only she could see. "Every year I asked him to let me go, and every year he refused."

"Him?"

"Your grandfather," Cornelia said.

"Why did you need his permission?"

"The bastard liked to keep us all under his thumb," Honeysuckle said. "In his mind, he was still the lord and we his servants."

"And how come you always call him 'the bastard'?" Sharon took in her surroundings, searching out an escape route.

Linda touched her friend's hand. "Because he disowned his daughter and you. Because he wouldn't allow his wife to visit you and your mother in Canada. Because he died drunk and miserable, just the way he lived."

"I can see you want to leave." Cornelia put her hand on the back of her granddaughter's chair. "I'm asking you to stay a little longer. Have some breakfast before you fly away. I'd like to get to know you a bit."

"You have no right to ask anything of me! I found the letters after my mother died. The letters she wrote to you! The letters returned unopened! She was dying, and you wouldn't even answer her letters!" Sharon felt herself finding a focus for the rage over the loss of her mother. "You know, the last few days before she died, she kept asking for you. She was delirious most of the time, but she hadn't forgotten you!"

"You were with her when she died?" Cornelia asked.

"Yes. The last week was a nightmare." Sharon looked at her grandmother, who was beginning to weep.

"I was so afraid she died alone. Where is she buried?" Cornelia asked.

"Calgary. Queen's Park." The day of the burial came back to Sharon. Its stark reality. The warm hand of the sun on her face. The faces of her neighbours and friends. "It was a beautiful day. I know it sounds crazy, but it was. The birds were singing."

"You know, your grandfather beat Cornelia when she said she was going to see your mother before she died," Honeysuckle said.

"What?" Sharon asked.

"Put Cornelia in the hospital, he did. Still, she was determined to leave. By the time Cornelia was well enough to travel, your mother was dead," Honeysuckle said.

"So you killed the bastard?" Sharon asked.

Honeysuckle and Cornelia looked at one another. They said nothing, but it was obvious some silent understanding passed between them. Linda and Sharon waited for an answer. None came.

Honeysuckle turned to Linda. "Your Aunt Rose lives in a cottage near White Waltham. You remember her?"

"Oh God. That woman never shuts her gob!" Linda gave her mother a horrified look. "You're not suggesting we move in with her?"

"The beauty of it is that Rose has moved in with her daughter while the son-in-law is away at sea. The two of you would have Rose's cottage to yourself. I'll ask, if you like," Honeysuckle said.

Linda looked at Sharon, who shrugged. "That would be great."

"All right," Linda said.

An hour later, Sharon checked on the port and starboard sides of the cockpit, then said "Clear!" and switched on.

Linda swung the Tiger Moth's propeller, stepped back, then moved around the wing after the engine caught.

Sharon eased the throttle forward. The engine coughed. She eased the throttle back. The engine smoothed itself out.

Linda climbed into the front cockpit and worked her way into the safety harness.

Sharon looked at the women standing by the gate at the rock wall. They stood close to one another. Honeysuckle wrapped an arm around Cornelia's shoulders. Sharon waved, and her grandmother smiled back.

Linda drummed the side of the fuselage fabric.

Sharon eased the throttle forward and swung the aircraft into the wind.

When the wheels skipped over the grass for the last time, she felt a familiar rush of joy. In the air, all that had happened today, and all that had happened in the last two years, fell away as they gained altitude.

Almost three hours later, Sharon smiled as the wheels and tailskid trimmed the grass at the end of the runway. As she taxied closer, she saw Bloggs waiting in his familiar pose, leaning against the hangar and smoking a cigarette. Sharon wondered if he had moved from there since they'd left this morning.

When the propeller stopped and the quiet was new, Bloggs said, "Not a bad landing for a bloody woman!"

"Bastard." Sharon thought she'd said the word under her breath, but could see from Bloggs's reaction that he'd heard.

Linda undid her straps and turned to look at her friend with an expression that said, *Now you've done it.*

"Washed out!" Bloggs spat. "Nobody talks like that to me! Especially not a fucking wo —"

"You there!" A woman stood in the shadow of the hangar door, where her voice was amplified.

Bloggs pointed at Sharon, his message clear: *I'm not finished with you.* Then he turned and said, "Who the hell are you?"

"Senior Commander Pauline Gower! And your name, sir?"

"Waverly Bloggs."

"I was about to offer these excellent pilots a position in the Air Transport Auxiliary. Can you think of any reason why these two might not be qualified to fly in the defense of England? Keep in mind I've just witnessed an exemplary three-point landing. I'm assuming you're responsible for what must have been their remarkable training?" Gower looked past Bloggs to Linda and Sharon, who stood beside the Tiger Moth.

"Umm. . ." Bloggs said.

"I'll take that as a yes. You two!" Gower waved Linda and Sharon closer.

They walked toward Gower, who had curly hair and appeared to be ten years older than either of them. "We've got a few things to discuss. I don't know if you are aware, but I've been put in charge of recruiting pilots for the ATA. Our initial base will be at White Waltham."

Sharon glanced at Linda. *How do you know so much about what's going on in this country?*

Gower said, "White Waltham is a small airfield close to London and many of the major airfields, like Duxford, Biggin Hill, Croydon, and Henley. So you'll be right in the middle of all of the action that is sure to come, and close to the fighter bases charged with the defense of Britain. I haven't got time to mess about. Here it is: Are the two of you interested in flying aircraft from assembly points and factories to the RAF airfields?"

# CHAPTER 2

**"Why *do* you get to fly one?"** Linda sipped her tea and left red lipstick on the rim. She handed another cup to Sharon. They sat out front of the green-roofed dispersal hut at White Waltham. It was a long, one-storey, chocolate-coloured building with white-trimmed windows. At one end, there was a hangar, half a cylinder, really, where the aircraft were stored and maintained.

The morning sun set its chin on the horizon.

Sharon listened to the birdsong. "Thanks." She took the tea and grimaced at the first sip.

"I know, it's disgusting. Still, you haven't answered the question."

Sharon spoke before thinking. "And you haven't answered my question about my grandmother. You could have warned me." She thought, *And did you just get to know me because my grandmother asked you to? When I look back on it, you became friendly with me almost right away.*

"We've been over that. Cornelia wanted it that way." Linda tried to hide behind her tea. "Who's giving us a lift in the air taxi?"

"I think it's Roger."

Linda groaned.

"And don't change the subject."

The dispersal door opened. Roger looked at the pilots. He squinted through overgrown grey eyebrows. There was a river system of red blood vessels on either cheek. "Ready?" He wiped the back of his hand across his mouth.

Sharon poured her tea onto the ground and wondered if it would kill the grass.

Linda set her cup on the windowsill. "Off we go."

They followed Roger and the formidable odour of sweat and alcohol. He was having a difficult time negotiating his way over the apparently uneven ground.

Sharon looked down at the carefully manicured grass. She glanced sideways at Linda.

Her friend mimed taking a drink, rolled her eyes, and staggered.

"You feeling okay?" Sharon called out to Roger.

"Perfectly fine." Roger opened the back door of the Anson. It was a camouflaged, twin-engined, humpbacked tail-dragger with delusions of sophistication. He threw his parachute inside and followed it.

Sharon went next. The smell of sour beer filled the confined space.

"Don't worry, I'll get you there safe." Roger looked over his shoulder, then made his way up to the cockpit.

A sulfurous stench filled the cabin.

Sharon looked over her shoulder.

Linda looked bemused, then distressed. "Wasn't me." She glanced ahead at Roger. "Let's hurry up and get seated so he can get moving. That way there'll be a draft running through this crate." Linda closed the door and stuck her nose in the crook of her elbow.

Sharon thought, *I don't know what's worse: Roger's terrible flying or his beer farts.*

Linda tapped Sharon on the shoulder. "Why do you get to go to Castle Bromwich to pick up a Spitfire?"

"I don't know." *Maybe if I change the subject.* "Where is Castle Bromwich?"

"Huge factory northeast of London, near Birmingham, but you already know that. You're just trying to distract me." Linda leaned back, crossed her arms under her breasts, and shook her head. "Bloody unfair."

o **Sharon approached the Spitfire** with more than a little apprehension. *Don't lose your nerve. Not now, not here!* She belched, put her left hand on the wing, and promptly threw up onto the grass.

The fitter looked the other way as she wiped her mouth.

She walked around the wing. There was the scent of fresh paint and oil.

She swallowed hard and lifted her parachute onto the wing before stepping onto the wing root and climbing to the open cockpit door. She balanced there, hooked up the harnesses of her parachute, and climbed inside. The fitter closed the door and helped her strap on the Sutton safety harness. "Did anyone warn you about the Spit's habit of pulling to one side after take-off? Propeller torque, you know."

Sharon nodded and smiled up at the man, who smiled back.

"And don't forget about the sewage pond over there." He pointed off the end of the runway. "Try not to end up in there. The rescue crews are a little reluctant to go in after pilots who end up in that mess."

"I'll do my best." She looked at the gauges and recited the routine she'd memorized during weeks of training for this moment.

When the engine fired, it belched exhaust past the open cockpit. She opened the throttle and the Merlin smoothed out. She followed her training, taxied out, did her run up, checked the windsock, checked for traffic, and opened the throttle. The acceleration was like no other aircraft she'd ever flown before. Ready for the torque of the propeller, she countered with opposite rudder. The tail lifted. The wings bit the air. The wheels left the ground.

She touched the brakes, then retracted the undercarriage. At five hundred feet, she closed the canopy and brought up the flaps. The Spitfire was clean and alive. She leveled off at one thousand feet, set the propeller at coarse pitch, and saw that she was cruising at nearly two hundred and fifty knots. It seemed like only minutes later that she found herself just south of London, circling the legendary RAF airfield at Biggin Hill. She looked down at the runway on top of a hill. Sharon throttled back, then lowered the flaps and undercarriage. Reluctantly, she guided the Spitfire to land into the wind.

After signing over her aircraft, Sharon followed the scent of coffee to the canteen and sat down near the outside wall of the tent. She'd spotted four pilots gathered along the inside at a table next to the canvas wall. Their conversation was easy to hear. The voices were a mélange of accents from Scotland, England and New Zealand.

"Anyone see that wee slip of a girl deliver the new Spit this morning?"

"Quite the looker, that one. Brown hair, blue eyes, petite."

"Landed like she knew what she was doing."

"There's not much of that happening around here these days. Wee pups of pilots who can barely change their nappies, let alone fly a Spitfire. We're so short of pilots, she'll be fightin' soon."

"Rather fly with her than the one the skipper sent packin' yesterday."

"The stupid bastard would na follow orders."

"Malan's got his own rules. He expects you to follow 'em and expects you to do your job."

"I know. I know. Watch out for the Hun in the sun."

"Don't shoot 'til you see the whites of their eyes."

"And he uses the finger-four formation instead of line astern."

"Typical bloody colonial, making his own rules to suit the situation."

"Would ye like to join one of those other squadrons and be arse end Charlie?"

Sharon sipped her coffee in the brief silence, worrying they'd caught onto the fact that she was eavesdropping.

"Not on your life! I'd like to survive this bloody war!"

"Skipper sent another one packin' this mornin'."

"That opinionated bastard with three last names?"

"That's 'im. Would na want him watchin' my back. So busy followin' the RAF rules of engagement, he'd get me killed. One of Hitler's secret weapons, that one."

"Skipper's our secret weapon."

"Him and O'Malley."

Sharon stopped breathing. She closed her eyes to concentrate on the reply.

"Bloody magician, that one."

"Bloody-minded Irishman, if you ask me."

"Ever have your guns jam in the middle of a dogfight?"

Another silence.

"Ever have an engine failure?"

Another silence.

"I thank my lucky stars every day for that bloody-minded Irishman. Talk to the pilots in other squadrons, and they'll tell ye what it's like to find yourself in the middle of a mess of Messerschmitt 109s with jammed guns. That does na happen here because O'Malley and Malan will nay have fools workin' around our Spitfires."

There was the sound of a twin-engined aircraft on finals.

Sharon looked up and spotted a sleek biplane settling onto the grass. She recognized the Dragon Rapide that was to be her ride back.

"Yer ride's here, lassie."

She saw a smiling ginger-haired sergeant pilot peering at her through a gap in the tent's fabric.

He said, with his no-nonsense Scottish accent, "Keep your wits about ye. There'll be Germans nearby, and they don't take the time to find out whether you're a woman or a man. They'll kill ye given half a fookin' chance."

o *"So, you met him?"* Linda sat across from Sharon in a pub near White Waltham, where the heavy scent of fermenting beer was almost as thick as the tobacco smoke.

"No. The pilots were talking about him." Sharon looked around. Some of the patrons were eating steak and kidney pie, others were smoking, and all were hefting a pint or four. She saw all of this through a haze of smoke. The ceiling was so low, it had nowhere to sit but in front of her face. Her eyelids felt like sandpaper. "Are you finished?"

Linda chewed the last forkful of her supper.

Sharon thought, *You eat like a man and weigh maybe one hundred and twenty-five pounds. How do you do that?*

"I don't know. I've always had a healthy appetite." Linda stood. "Let's talk some more on the way back."

*Did I say that out loud? She's reading my mind again.* "Fair enough."

Outside, Sharon inhaled fresher air. The blackout made the stars brighter. She sniffed her uniform jacket and found it stank of cigarette smoke and sweat.

"No drinking. No smoking. What kind of Canadian are you?"

Sharon turned and anger lit her from within. She was greeted with Linda's smile. The anger was extinguished. "My mother died from the one, and my grandfather abused everyone because of the other. By the way, how do you read my mind?"

"Your face is as easy to read as the morning headlines." Linda linked her arm through Sharon's.

Sharon felt flushed with embarrassment, as well as something unfamiliar, unnamed.

Linda said, "You know, when I found out who you were, I told my mother, and my father looked into you."

"What is MI5, anyway?"

"Intelligence. Now, that has to stay between you and me. It's all so hush-hush, you know." Linda did not smile.

"Really?"

Linda pulled Sharon's elbow and stopped them. "Really. We even have an official secrets act now."

"Does that mean that what we talk about stays between us?"

"From now on, if you like. I told my mother about you because she took care of Cornelia after your grandfather beat her. They became close again. My mother told Cornelia about you coming to England after the bastard died."

"How did he die?" Sharon asked.

The silence went on for more than a minute. Linda asked, "How did you find out about O'Malley?"

"My mother told me about him a couple of weeks before she died. She'd tracked him down through one of her old friends — someone who had worked for Cornelia for years. She gave me the letter, but the signature was blacked out. That's how I knew where he was." Sharon had a flashback of her mother's skeletal body in the hospital bed.

"Who do you think was your mother's old friend?" Linda asked.

Sharon tried to read Linda's expression through the darkness. "It was Honeysuckle! She was the one who wrote my mother."

"Yes. Your mother and my mother were friends from childhood. Honeysuckle met your father on several occasions," Linda said.

Sharon shook the image of her mother's last emaciated days out of her mind. "I want to meet him."

"Yes, I suppose."

Sharon heard Linda's reluctant tone. "Well?"

"You know that there is risk involved?"

"Of course," Sharon said. "What's your father like?"

"Kind of distant. Smart. Lives in his own little world." Linda touched Sharon's arm.

"I want to meet my father and find out for myself what he's like."

# CHAPTER 3
## [ JUNE 1940 ]

**"We have a twenty-four-hour leave coming up.** Would you like to come home with me? My father will be there. And Honeysuckle will be sure to prepare a feast." Linda looked over her cup of tea. Her eyes were smiling and awake, even though the sun was just leaning with its elbows on the eastern horizon.

"Another meeting with Cornelia?" Sharon felt an anxious butterfly stirring in her belly. "It's a long way to go for one day."

"That's already taken care of. We make a delivery to Church Fenton. It's near Leeds, close to Ilkley. A car will be waiting for us." Linda pointed her finger at the dispersal hut as an elegant, white-haired, and clean-shaven man stepped outside. His hair was tinted orange by the rising sun. He looked in their direction and pointed. His name was Mr. Green — no one seemed to know his first name — and the way he fussed over "his" pilots had earned him the nickname of Mother.

Sharon stood up. "I wonder what Mother has for us this morning?"

"You seem a little off lately. What's the matter?" Linda asked.

"Did my mother write more than one letter to Honeysuckle?" Sharon looked directly at her friend.

"She wrote several, actually." Linda tapped the bench with her palm, indicating that Sharon should sit back down.

Sharon remained standing. "She must have been writing letters while she was in the hospital. Did you read them?"

"Yes, Honeysuckle showed them to me. You must understand that she and Leslie were very close. They remained in contact over the years. When Leslie became ill, she wrote to my mother more often. Your mother was worried about what would happen to you after she died. Honeysuckle shared the letters with me. In the last letter, Leslie said that you might be coming to England. That you had talked about finding your father. She was worried about how you would be received by her family. So my mother asked my father to watch for your name on the passenger manifests of ships arriving from Canada. In wartime, men like my father have access to all sorts of information." Linda reached into the pocket of her flight suit and pulled out a pack of cigarettes.

Sharon watched as her friend struck a match and lit up.

Linda inhaled. "So, by now, you've sussed out the fact that our initial meeting was not accidental." She looked at her friend.

Sharon said, "Your father told you where to find me?"

Linda nodded. "My mother and Cornelia wanted to make sure that you were all right — that you would be safe. The fact that we're both pilots made it easy."

"It all seems so calculated."

"It certainly was at first." Linda exhaled a cloud of smoke.

"And now?" Sharon was afraid of what the answer might be.

Linda picked at the filter of her cigarette with her thumbnail. "We're friends, aren't we?"

o **"When the French surrender, we'll be on our own."** Linda's father sat in the garden on the east side of their home. Harry's hair was thin on top. It was more silver than red now. Behind his glasses, there was tired worry in his blue eyes. He sat across from Sharon and Linda. Honeysuckle stepped out of the house and walked toward them.

Sharon thought, *They always seem to avoid talking about Michael. I wonder if there is any news?*

Linda looked at her father. "Have we got anything left to fight Jerry with?"

Harry glared at her. "What have you heard?"

Linda said, "The pilots who've come back from France talk about what it was like. How the Nazis blitzed their way through Europe. I've got ears!"

Sharon added, "After a delivery, it's impossible not to hear the talk. Many say the Luftwaffe has more aircraft and more experience. Hitler has been rebuilding his air force for years, and the RAF has a long way to go to catch up."

Harry smiled. "Perhaps the pair of you should work for MI5 in London. Your assessment is remarkably accurate."

"Are you going to answer the question, dear?" Honeysuckle sat down at the table next to her husband. She looked across at Sharon. "Cornelia said she'd be happy to join us for lunch."

Sharon nodded in reply. She felt tension's grip behind her navel.

"Churchill got the wrong number stuck in his mind." Harry looked at his daughter.

Sharon noticed that Harry had a habit of taking his time revealing juicy bits of information. It often took a series of questions before he would get to the point.

"Sharon and I have already flown to most of the RAF airfields. We've seen the situation. We're not idiots, you know."

Harry's face was redder than his hair. Honeysuckle put her hand on his.

Harry took a breath. "Winston has the number twenty-five stuck in his mind. He thinks we need that many squadrons to defend England. Dowding is the head of the Royal Air Force. He repeatedly told Churchill that the absolute minimum is fifty-two. On the positive side, some of our pilots are still straggling back from the continent. There are even some Polish flyers who are forming a squadron. It seems clear, however, that we're going to be below the fifty-two squadron minimum. And it's absolutely clear that the Luftwaffe has us outnumbered almost three to two. When France surrenders — and I'm saying when, not if — Hitler will feel the need to defeat the RAF before he attempts an invasion of England. If we're lucky, he'll put Goering in charge." He gave Sharon a worried glance.

Sharon covered her mouth with her right hand. *I can keep my mouth shut. Don't worry.* "Why is that?"

Harry nodded at her. "Goering is more concerned about the style of his uniform than his tactics."

Honeysuckle smiled.

Linda shook her head and said, "You don't have to concern your-self about Sharon. She and I talk about most things. And she knows how to keep a secret."

Honeysuckle looked at Sharon. "It appears you have picked a very bad time to come to England."

*I've been thinking the same thing,* she thought. "What are our chances?"

Harry looked out into the garden. "It's hard to say. Assembling an invasion fleet is a complex undertaking. We still have a strong navy, and our latest fighters are a match for the Luftwaffe's best. The problem is that we do not have enough Spitfires and Hurricanes, or even enough pilots to fly them."

"So the situation is desperate?" Honeysuckle asked.

"Well, not exactly." Harry reached for a cup of tea.

"Well? You make it sound desperate," Linda said.

"We can track aircraft as they approach our coast." Harry looked around the garden, checking to see who might be listening. A pair of blackbirds sat chirping at one another on a nearby branch.

"Yes, of course, the Observer Corps." Linda wagged her finger at her father to scold him for revealing information they already knew.

Harry set his tea down and shook his head. "No, it's something new. Something quite different altogether."

"So are you going to tell us or not?" Linda stood to force her father's hand.

"We will have advanced warning of the Luftwaffe as they form up over France and head this way."

"Sounds fanciful," Honeysuckle said.

"Sounds like the Druids are involved." Linda rolled her eyes.

*So that's what those towers built up and down the coastline are for,* Sharon thought.

Harry turned away from his daughter and toward Sharon. "You're a bit of a mystery. You arrive here off a ship and end up flying for the ATA. Where did you learn how to fly?"

Sharon looked back at him and replied without thinking. "My mother was a secretary for a construction company in Calgary. The owner and his wife took us under their wing. Their children were all grown up, so, on the weekends, we'd often go to their ranch south of the city."

Sharon looked around the table. Harry, Linda, and Honeysuckle were leaning forward to hear every word.

Linda said, "Go on."

"My mother's boss, Douglas, had an airplane he used for work. He'd fly around the country looking at various construction sites. He saw that I was fascinated with flying. When I could reach the controls, he began to teach me." Sharon thought back to those flights, those weekends and summer holidays she would look forward to the way she looked forward to Christmas morning.

"How old were you when you began flying?" Honeysuckle asked.

Sharon shrugged and looked at them. "Ten. I had a license by the time I was seventeen. Not all of my time in the air is in my logbook. I've got well over twelve hundred hours of official flying time."

"That certainly answers a few questions," Linda said.

"Like what?" Sharon asked.

"Like why you're such a good pilot. Like why you can fly better than all of the people who trained us. Why you fly at least as well as the pilots in the RAF." Linda chuckled.

"What's so funny?" Harry asked.

Linda pointed at her friend. "The fighter pilots often can't believe it when she lands. Most of them have an eye for the finer points of flying. Their mouths fall open when she steps down from the wing. Some admire her ability. Others, well. . ."

"Well?" Honeysuckle asked.

"I think some are jealous that a woman flies as well as Sharon does." Linda looked at her father. "In fact, better than most of them."

"You liked this Douglas?" Harry asked.

Sharon thought for a minute. "He never asked why I didn't have a father. He just accepted me. He treated me like an equal, like a friend. Douglas taught me that I could be a match for anyone, and that because I was good at flying, there were lots of other things I could do. Flying his Staggerwing gave me confidence. And he taught me how to shoot skeet."

"A Staggerwing! You flew a Beechcraft Staggerwing?" Linda hit the table with her palm.

Sharon sat back. "Yes, that's what Douglas had parked in his hangar."

"So, at ten years old, you flew a Beechcraft Staggerwing?" Linda looked at her father and shook her head. "You've been flying a performance aircraft since you were ten!" Linda's expression and her tone of voice told them all that some great secret had been revealed.

"You're saying that it's unfair that I learned to become a good pilot?" Sharon felt anger leaping over logic.

"No. It's just her awkwardly uncivil way of saying she admires your flying ability." Honeysuckle stood, put her hands on her hips, and leaned back with her eyes closed and her face to the sun. "Come on, Harry, you've got to do your duty." She winked at her husband.

Linda blushed.

Sharon thought, *What was that wink all about?*

Harry and Honeysuckle got up and walked into the house.

"What's got your knickers in a knot?" Linda asked.

Sharon looked at her friend while cocking her head to one side.

Linda went to say something, stopped, and then said, "I know! It's me who's upset. It's just that my parents act as though Michael was never here. They seem to think that ignoring his disappearance will make everything all right!" She used a handkerchief tucked up her sleeve to wipe tears away.

*Yes, it is strange.*

"It's that stiff upper lip! It makes me so furious! I can't pretend that everything is going to be okay!" Linda stood up.

Sharon followed as Linda walked down into the garden, along a stone path, and into a stand of trees. She stopped and stood with her hands holding her elbows. The sun dappled her head and shoulders. A breeze shifted light and shadow. Her red hair changed shades.

Sharon moved alongside her friend.

"Michael and I used to spend hours playing here among the trees. We felt safe here. Now it feels like nothing is safe anymore. Bloody Nazis!" Linda looked up into the branches of the trees. "This oak tree was his favourite. He loved to climb it. He'd try to get me to follow, but I never would."

"How come?"

"I'm afraid of heights." Linda turned to face her. "Isn't that hysterical?"

"Flying is completely different, actually." Sharon lifted her chin, tapped it with the back of her hand, and winked at Linda.

Linda's laughter was sharp and short. "Come along. Your grandmother will be here soon. She might walk into the house and catch my parents *in flagrante delicto.*"

*What are you talking about?* "What do you mean?"

"Making the beast with two backs." Linda looked flustered.

"Speak English!" Sharon followed Linda back to the house.

They found Cornelia sitting at the table in the back garden. She stood as the two young women stepped into the open. "Oh, good. I was afraid I'd arrived at the wrong time."

Sharon almost laughed out loud.

"No, not really," Linda said. "My parents should be out momentarily."

As she spoke, Honeysuckle stepped outside, followed by Harry, who carried a tray with tea and sandwiches. Both were smiling and looking a little flushed.

Within minutes, all were seated around the table with a cup of tea and a pyramid of sandwiches within reach.

"Marmaduke and his family are arriving next week for an extended visit." Cornelia made no attempt to hide her excitement.

Honeysuckle sipped her tea before saying, "How *nice.*"

To Sharon's ears, Honeysuckle's tone said that Marmaduke's visit was very far from being nice.

Linda said, "Yes, quite a few people from London are making extended visits to the countryside." She stuffed a cucumber sandwich into her mouth as if hoping to stop herself from saying more.

Cornelia carried on as if she hadn't heard. "I haven't seen the grand-children since last summer, when they stayed for a month."

Sharon felt a pang of jealousy at the mention of cousins she had never known. *They're nothing to do with me.*

"Nothing like an imminent invasion to bring a family together," Linda said.

Harry glared at her. "It will be good for you to see the grand-children."

Cornelia touched Sharon's hand. "I hope you'll be able to visit, so I can introduce them to you."

"Sharon wouldn't miss it!" Linda turned to her friend. "And nei-ther would I!"

Honeysuckle said, "Linda, would you help me bring out dessert?" She stood up.

Linda smiled. "Of course, Mother."

Sharon gathered plates and followed them into the kitchen.

Honeysuckle closed the door behind Sharon and said to her daugh-ter, "What is wrong with you?"

Linda said, "You can all live in your fantasy worlds, where we never deal with reality, never mention Michael's name, and never say how Marmaduke blamed his mother for the old bastard's death, but some of us have to live in the real world! There is a war on, and Mar-maduke is moving in with his mother to save his skin and lay claim to the estate!"

Sharon looked at Honeysuckle.

"That's true." Honeysuckle faced Sharon. "Your uncle, unfortu-nately, is much like his father."

The phone rang.

Linda picked it up, listened, then hung up. "Sharon, we've been called back."

Sharon heard relief in her friend's voice.

o **Within thirty minutes,** Sharon and Linda were in the back seat of Cornelia's Rolls-Royce, her chauffeur at the wheel. Sharon looked out the window at stone walls, gardens, and thatched roofs. *This*

*is my first summer in England and my second ride in a Rolls-Royce.*
It felt remarkably similar to a Buick she'd had a ride in once.

Linda looked out the other side.

After half an hour, Sharon said, "Did they say why we're being called back?"

Linda shook her head. "Mother wouldn't say. It was all very cryptic." She made eye contact with Sharon and glanced at the driver. The message was clear: anything said would be reported back.

Sharon looked ahead and saw the eyes of the driver studying her. She thought for a moment, trying to remember the driver's face, and found she could not.

Sharon passed the rest of the trip in silence, memorizing the route, noting that the road signs had all been taken down in order to make navigation difficult for an invading army.

As they approached the airport, more military vehicles and men in uniform were visible. One group marched in the opposite direction with broomsticks instead of rifles on their shoulders.

Sharon saw a blend of anger, determination, and fear on their faces.

# CHAPTER 4
## [ JULY 1940 ]

**"What's the matter with you?"** Linda sat behind Sharon in the Anson, their ride to the first delivery of the day.

Roger was up front, concentrating on his instruments. It appeared his frequent belching was an attempt at holding down a breakfast of greasy sausages he called bangers.

Sharon looked out her window for a glimpse of the ground. There was the hint of green treetops disappearing into a world of grey cloud. "I was hoping to fly today."

"Today, tomorrow, next week, don't worry — you'll get back to Biggin Hill. I just hope. . ." Linda put her hand over her mouth.

"What? Spit it out!" Sharon glared at her friend. The Anson hit a patch of rough air. She grabbed the back of the seat in front of her. The wings flexed. The airframe groaned.

Linda looked around for a paper bag. "I hope your father isn't a disappointment." Her eyes rolled and she swallowed hard.

"Here." Sharon pulled a paper bag from her coverall pocket.

Linda grabbed the bag and held it over her mouth and nose. "Don't you ever get airsick?"

Sharon shook her head. She looked out the window. A railway line ran about five hundred feet below the aircraft. "It's usually tension that does it to me. I think we're getting close."

They felt and heard Roger throttle back.

Sharon looked ahead, but couldn't see much out of the cockpit windows because of Roger's hulking frame, so she looked out through the side. *I hope he wasn't drunk last night. And I hope he isn't drunk right now.*

The flaps extended.

The wheels thumped down.

They passed through dense cloud and into the open. She could see the approach to the runway.

There was a bump of turbulence.

Linda threw up.

The wheels kissed the runway.

The cabin filled with the sweet-sour stink of vomit.

"Your stop, Canada!" Roger said.

When she climbed out the side door, Sharon had her gear in one hand, and Linda's airsick bag in the other. She moved away from the wash of the propellers tugging at her coveralls. For a moment, Linda's ashen features were framed in the rectangular window. The engines revved, and she was gone.

Sharon walked toward the dispersal hut.

A group of pilots waited near the canteen, looking at the clouds, sipping tea, and munching on white bread sandwiches.

*Bully beef.* Sharon's stomach turned at the thought of what passed for meat in England. She looked at the bag in her hand. *Oh, no.*

"Wrong time of the month? A bun in the oven, perhaps?"

Sharon turned and saw Bloggs' smug face as all the pilots turned to gauge her reaction.

She felt the weight of the bag.

"Morning sickness or just down a pint?" Bloggs was encouraged by the reactions to his first comments.

Sharon lifted the bag and considered throwing it in his face. She walked closer to the men. The woman in the canteen frowned from overtop of the heads of the men.

Bloggs turned to one of the other pilots. "There's a rumour that Churchill might have to put the war on hold because female pilots are complaining about flying when they have their time of the month."

Sharon smiled. "Here, Mr. Bloggs, this is for you."

The young woman in the canteen hid a smile behind her hand.

Bloggs was silent. He kept his hands at his sides.

"Don't feel like a light lunch?" Sharon lifted the bag for all to see. "Because what's in here is better than what you're eating right now!"

One of the pilots laughed. The others followed.

"Oi! Sharon. There's a priority delivery!" Walter ran things at Castle Bromwich, the Spitfire factory. His round face wore a smile as he waved a chit at Sharon.

She set the bag on the table behind Bloggs, turned, and walked toward Walter.

When she was close, Walter said, "Biggin Hill."

Her stomach lurched. She took the piece of paper.

o *An hour later,* she was turning on finals for her approach to Biggin Hill. An airfield surrounded by trees and green fields (including one that was red) of various shapes. The clouds had lifted to two thousand feet. Still, the sun could not penetrate the overcast.

*I wonder if I'll see my father this time.* She looked ahead and saw a red Very light flare as it hit the top of its arc.

Sharon checked to see if the wheels were down. "Gear down."

She looked ahead. Another red Very light screamed up from the control tower.

The peripheral vision in her left eye caught a speck of motion. She turned her head.

A pair of Messerschmitt 109s streaked along the underbelly of the overcast sky. The green-grey Nazi single-engined fighters flew side by side. Their left wings dipped as they turned to attack her from behind.

She glanced at the overcast. *Damn! Not enough time for me to climb and disappear into the cloud!*

Sharon looked at the hangars below, then over her shoulder at the yellow-nosed enemy fighters.

She opened the throttle gradually. *No! Don't retract the gear. They'll know you've spotted them.* The altimeter read two hundred feet.

She looked in the mirror just above her head. The yellow nose and one wing of the lead Messerschmitt were visible.

Sharon looked ahead. *Almost there! The timing has to be perfect.* She squeezed her shoulders together and crouched lower in front of the armour plating.

She turned right, added throttle, and aimed for the gap between the grey curved roofs of a pair of Belfast hangars.

Tracer bullets appeared on her left.

There was a glimpse of upturned faces in the wide-open mouth of the first hangar door.

The Spitfire had its right wing within ten feet of the ground as Sharon hauled the control stick over, was sucked into her seat by the violence of the maneuver, and passed between the concrete walls of the hangars.

Sharon waited for the impact of German cannon shells. She passed beyond the hangars, over a stand of trees, and down, 'til she was ten feet over a pasture. A pair of startled calves darted for their mother.

Sharon lifted up over another stand of trees and turned right, following a roadway and a stone wall. Then she turned right again. A glance above told her the sky was clear. Another told her there was no one in her mirror.

She turned right and checked to make sure her wheels were down.

Ahead, a green Very light flare streaked into the sky, reached the top of its arc, and dove down.

A smudge of oily black smoke rose up beyond the hangars.

She throttled back. In moments, the main wheels kissed the runway. She taxied on two wheels until she was close to a hangar and throttled back.

The engine crackled at idle and she looked in the rear-view mirror to see if the yellow-nosed 109s were attacking.

The sky was empty.

When Sharon shut the engine down, she waited in the silence and looked at the faces of the men who came to examine her aircraft for damage. One man stood away from the Spitfire and circled. When he came to the right wing, he stopped and looked at Sharon.

A frown spread lines across his forehead and created a V at the crown.

Sharon undid her harness and slid back the canopy. She opened the door and stepped out onto the wing.

"Lovely bit of flying, that," someone said.

She looked to her right. A fitter was pointing past her at the black smoke. "Jerry tried to follow you. Isn't that right, O'Malley?"

She stepped down onto the ground.

Sharon leaned against the wing when her knees began to shake. She looked at the balding man with a barrel chest and mechanic's arms.

O'Malley said, "Leslie?"

"My mother's name was Leslie. She emigrated to Canada and died last year. I came over here to meet my father." Sharon thought, *This is not how I planned for us to meet.*

The V in O'Malley's forehead deepened. His face turned red.

Sharon looked around her. The other men had turned their backs and were beginning to walk away.

"You almost got yourself killed!" O'Malley's voice echoed off the wall of the hangar and bounced back at them. "Have you ever seen a body after a crash like that?"

*Why is he yelling?* "Of course I haven't, you asshole!"

O'Malley moved in so close that his nose almost touched hers. His voice was nearly a whisper. "I may indeed be an asshole, but I'm also your father! Do you think I didn't know about you? I've heard rumours of you for years. I even got a letter from your mother before she died. Now I almost get to see you killed before my eyes because you aren't watching out for the bloody Nazis. Those bastards have become damn good at shooting down anyone who isn't paying attention! They're professionals, you know!"

Sharon's voice shook. "Well, I guess that makes me better than that Nazi professional, doesn't it?" She pointed in the direction of the crashed fighter.

"Come with me." O'Malley grabbed her by the elbow and pulled her around behind the hangar, toward the black smoke rising from the wreck of the Messerschmitt.

"What are you doing?" Sharon asked, even though she knew exactly what he was about to do. It looked like there were fewer than a hundred yards between them and the crash site.

"We're at war. There is a reality to war that you need to see."

"Oi!"

O'Malley stopped and turned.

An officer approached. He was wearing aviator sunglasses and a white turtleneck sweater. "What's so important that I had to interrupt a bloody good card game?"

There was a stink in the air. It wasn't just gasoline. *The last time I smelled that, I was at a ranch where they were branding cattle,* Sharon thought.

"This young woman outfoxed that poor bastard over there," O'Malley said.

"I'm not blind, O'Malley. The men back there say she's your daughter! This is not the way to show her what war is like. She won't thank you for it. Besides," he motioned in the direction of the crash, "it smells worse than it looks by now." The officer adjusted his sunglasses. "That was a lovely bit of flying, by the way. Used Jerry's speed against him. Think I might try that one sometime, given the right circumstances."

Sharon pulled her arm away from her father's grip. "Be my guest."

"Squadron Leader Malan, meet my daughter," O'Malley said.

"Sharon Lacey." She offered her hand. "I've already learned your ten commandments."

Malan stared at her then took her hand. "I bet you have. Understand one thing. Those bastards won't hesitate if they get the chance to shoot you down." He looked at Patrick. "O'Malley?"

"Sir?"

"I'm going to take a pair of our new pilots up for some practice. Both are green as grass. Get me three Spits ready." Malan turned and walked toward the dispersal hut.

O'Malley turned to Sharon. "Will you come and see me again?"

Sharon nodded. "Where will I find you next time I'm in the neighbourhood?"

"I'll be here."

o *"So you swore at him?"* Linda chewed while holding her free hand in front of her face. In the other, she held a greasy page of newsprint and the demolished remnants of her fish and chips. "Must be some quaint Canadian custom you've yet to explain to me."

Sharon began to say something; instead, she contemplated the wallpaper.

"Nothing to say?" Linda licked the fingers of her right hand. "I mean, you wait more than a year to meet someone, then get into an argument. I should have thought you would have prepared lots of other clever things to say."

*Sometimes, your British sense of humour escapes me*, she thought. "There's more to it than that, actually."

Linda leaned back in her chair. She sat across from Sharon in the living room of her Aunt Rose's cottage, located within walking distance of White Waltham. The same Aunt Rose who had gone to visit with her daughter's family while her son-in-law was off at sea. "I'm waiting."

"He was angry with me for not keeping my eyes open. The problem was my being preoccupied with what to say should I meet my father. So in a way, it was his fault I didn't spot the Messerschmitt 109s right away." Sharon remembered how red her father's face had gotten when she swore at him.

"What do you mean, you didn't spot the Messerschmitts right away?" Linda rolled the newspaper into a ball and looked for a place to toss it.

"A pair of Messerschmitts were hanging around the airfield, and they turned to get on my tail while I was landing."

Linda leaned forward in her chair. The newspaper dropped on the floor. "What?"

"Two Messerschmitts. Both had yellow noses." *How did I remember that?*

"How did you get away from them?" Linda was all ears now. There wasn't a hint of irony in her voice.

"I flew in between a pair of hangars just as the first one opened fire." Sharon remembered the panic, elation, and a remarkable clarity of thought that came with engaging the enemy fighters.

"And?"

"I circled around and landed." Sharon looked out the window, where day turned to dusk.

Linda shook her head. "And Jerry just let you go on your merry way?"

"By that time, the remaining 109 had run off."

"Remaining 109?"

"The one on my tail crashed. The wingman left after that." Sharon remembered the smell of burning flesh. The stink of Linda's greasy fish and chips caught at the back of her throat.

"You caused him to crash?"

"That's right. I turned. He tried to follow and he either went into a high-speed stall or clipped one of the hangar roofs. I'm not sure which."

"You outfoxed the Luftwaffe."

"Well, not the entire German air force. Just one pilot." Sharon swallowed as her mouth filled with saliva.

# CHAPTER 5

*"The longer we go with no news at all,* the more I think my brother's not coming home." Linda had her white flight suit zipped up just under her chin. Her legs were crossed and her hands were stuffed into her pockets.

Sharon stood next to the bench outside of the White Waltham dispersal hut. She tried to come up with a reply, but found herself unable to find the words.

Linda looked up at her friend. "You're still in a funk over that Jerry pilot, aren't you?"

"Yes." Sharon sat down beside Linda and handed her a cup of coffee.

"What are you upset about, exactly?" Linda held the cup out front with the little finger of her right hand pointing to the sky, where the first hint of sunrise brushed blue over black.

*I killed him. I smelled him burning in the wreckage.*

Linda crossed her right knee over her left and adopted a thinker's pose. "Is it because what's left of him would fit in a biscuit tin, or because he smelled a bit like fish and chips wrapped in yesterday's news?" She took a sip of tea and fluttered her eyelashes.

Sharon felt her rage ignite. "How can you joke about this? I knew what I was doing. I knew he couldn't follow me into a turn. I led him right into a trap! He's dead, and it feels horrible to know I caused it!"

Linda set her cup down on the bench beside her. She unzipped the top of her white coveralls, uncrossed her legs, exhaled, and leaned her back up against the rough wood of the wall. Linda looked up at the sky.

"I know what you're going to say!"

Linda continued looking up. "What is that? It doesn't sound like it has twin engines."

"That it was him or me!"

Linda looked south, listening to the drone of an approaching aircraft.

"Somehow, that doesn't make it right! He's dead and I'm alive. How is that right? Why are you ignoring me?"

Linda watched the approaching aircraft turning toward the airfield. "Sounds like our ride has arrived. What is it?" She pointed. "Just so you know, I'm glad you're alive. As for my tasteless sense of humour, I make no apologies."

Sharon squinted toward the southeast. The high-winged aircraft had its landing lights on. It was lit from beneath with the orange glow of a sun just beyond the horizon. "Lysander."

"Are you absolutely sure?"

Sharon looked again. "Yes."

"Let's see if you're right." Linda sipped her coffee and crossed one ankle over the other.

They watched the approaching aircraft, heard the pilot throttle back, and saw the flaps drop above the inverted U of its fixed undercarriage. The radial engine and dragonfly wings confirmed Sharon's identification.

After the Lysander landed and began to taxi toward the hangar, Linda said, "You're absolutely right, of course. You have remarkable vision. It's a good thing Jerry's vision wasn't as good as yours, because we might not be having this conversation if it was." She put her coffee down, stood, and walked toward the hangar.

Sharon followed. She watched the Lysander's propeller slow, stutter, and stop. *Why is the aircraft painted black?*

A silver-on-black Bentley saloon car poked its long nose out from the far side of the hangar. It parked next to the Lysander.

The morning light painted the scene in shadow. The pilot slid the forward canopy back. The rear canopy opened.

The driver of the Bentley opened his door. "What made you decide to land here?"

The pilot pulled off his flying helmet, revealing scarred, mottled skin on the left side of his face. "Tangmere is fogged in. In fact, the entire south coast is socked in. My orders were to proceed here as a secondary airfield." He pointed his thumb at his passenger. "They want him in London right away. And White Waltham is close by."

The man in the rear cockpit stood up and lifted his legs over the side. He was dressed in a black coat and baggy black pants. Sharon thought, *He looks like he's from France.*

Linda gave a start.

Sharon sensed Linda's attention focusing on the passenger, who was sliding down the side of the Lysander to stand on the tarmac.

The passenger door of the Bentley opened. "Come on, get your finger out! We haven't got all day!"

Linda stepped forward.

The Frenchman approached the men in the car. *He's kind of handsomely familiar.*

"Michael!" Linda said.

The Frenchman turned in her direction. He stood still as he recognized her.

"You bastard!" Linda moved forward.

Sharon heard a metallic click.

Michael turned to face the beefy men standing next to the Bentley. One of them stepped forward with his hand inside his coat. "For Christ's sake, put that away!" Michael moved toward Linda. He was a head taller, with strawberry blonde hair and blue eyes.

She ran at him and struck him just under the ribs with her closed fist. "We thought you were dead! Why didn't you send word?"

Michael was a windless kite crumpling to the ground as his knees failed him.

One of the bodyguards grabbed Linda's arms and pulled her back. She promptly crushed his instep with her heel. He howled and released her.

The other bodyguard reached for Linda. Sharon kicked him in the kneecap. He folded.

"That's quite enough, ladies." Linda and Sharon looked at the pilot, who was leveling a revolver at them. The pilot kept his eyes on Linda while pointing the pistol at the bodyguards. "I take it you're either a Nazi spy or a relative."

Michael managed to gasp out, "She's my sister."

"Ah, siblings." The pilot uncocked the revolver and slipped it back into its holster. "A family reunion, then." He rubbed at a phantom left ear with the back of his hand. All that was left was scar tissue and a hole in the side of his head. "Who do I need to kill for a cup of coffee?"

"I couldn't send word. Not even to Father. The continent is a shambles." Michael rubbed his belly as he stood.

"I could use another cup of coffee," Sharon said.

"That's your justification?" Linda asked.

"You're Canadian, then?" the pilot asked.

"Look around you. Put it together, Linda! No one is supposed to know I'm alive," Michael said.

"That's right, the prairies." Sharon tried to follow two conversations at once.

"Will you shut up? I'm talking to my brother!" Linda said to the pilot and Sharon before turning back to Michael. "You're a spy? Then Father would have to know about it!"

The pilot moved closer to Sharon. "They're going to be a while, and I need you to show me where the coffee is. It's all I've thought about since leaving France. By the way, my name is Richard." He took Sharon by the elbow.

"Just a moment, young lady," one of the beefy men said. "You've assaulted representatives of His Majesty. You're under arrest."

Richard laughed. "Like hell she is! If you do that, I'll make sure the entire service finds out that all it took was a pair of schoolgirls in flight suits to take care of a couple of England's so-called commandos!"

Michael put his arm around Linda's shoulder.

She pushed him away.

He persisted. "I'm sorry."

Linda began to weep.

Sharon said, "Linda will need a cup, too."

The mood of the commandos didn't improve even after Richard handed each a cup of coffee. They insisted that Michael and Linda remain out of sight in the back seat of the Bentley. The driver checked his watch every thirty seconds, then glared at Sharon.

Sharon glanced at the scars on Richard's face as he leaned against the Bentley's bonnet.

He said, "It happened a year before the war started. I got out of the wreckage a moment late and was burned on the one side. There's a new hospital being started up at East Grinstead for survivors like me. Whoever designed Hurricanes and Spitfires decided the best place for the fuel tank was right in front of the cockpit. The surgeons at East Grinstead will be expecting lots of customers like me with their faces and hands burned."

"Sorry. I didn't mean to stare." Sharon watched as Linda leaned against her brother's shoulder in the back seat of the Bentley.

"Don't be sorry. I'm still alive. A few of my friends have died already. I feel quite fortunate, to tell you the truth." Richard took a sip of coffee.

The driver opened the door of the car. "Time to go!"

The other commando flipped the remains of his coffee onto the grass and opened Linda's door. "We're off."

Linda stepped out of the car. She wrapped her arms around her shoulders and tucked her chin to her chest.

Sharon hugged her friend.

"Fucking war!" Linda wiped her nose on the sleeve of her flying suit. "Fucking war takes everything away. My own brother can't even tell us he's alive." She looked at Sharon. "Then you have to deal with what happens when someone else dies so that you can survive."

"Where did you learn to defend yourself?" Richard asked.

Linda smiled. "My brother taught me."

Richard turned to Sharon. "And you?"

"My mother."

Linda said, "Those two bastards stole our coffee cups!"

*Now's not a good time to ask her about Michael,* Sharon thought.

o "*Quick, before he changes his mind.* We've got a late delivery to Leeds, and a car will be waiting for us when we get there to take us to Ilkley. Our ride back is at ten o'clock tomorrow morning. Hurry!" Linda threw a change of clothes into her shoulder bag.

Sharon stood up and stuffed her feet into her flying boots. "I've done five deliveries already today."

"Look, you stay here if you like. I have to talk with my mother. She has to know Michael is alive. He told me I couldn't tell her over the phone or by letter. He neglected to say anything about telling her face to face. I'll be damned if I'll keep all of the secrets my parents have kept the same way their parents did." Linda stepped into the hallway and out the front door.

*What the hell does that mean?* "Hang on!" Sharon took the time to lock the front door, then worked her arms into her Irvin jacket. Her boots scrubbed over the gravel. She looked at the horizon and estimated they had ninety minutes of sunlight remaining.

When they reached the airfield, Sharon saw an oversized humpbacked white biplane parked near a hangar. She scanned the rest of the airfield for other aircraft. "What is it?"

Linda stepped up onto the bottom wing. "Swordfish."

"What fish?"

Linda wheeled around and pointed. "Swordfish! We complete the first leg of its delivery to Scapa Flow. Thank God we don't have to fly it all the way up there. Come on, I've got the chit in my pocket."

*This thing looks like it was built for the last war,* Sharon thought as she completed the walk around. "It looks like a school bus with wings!" The plane smelled of oil, gasoline and dope — a flammable concoction. She had a flashback of Richard's scarred face. "And where is Scapa Flow?"

Linda sat in the cockpit and began reading the page on the Swordfish. "It's a naval base on an island north of Scotland."

Sharon climbed into the middle cockpit.

"Clear!" Linda started the engine and throttled back. When she was settled in, Sharon tapped Linda's shoulder.

Three minutes later, they were airborne and headed northeast.

Sharon was glad she brought her goggles. Engine exhaust and oil blew back into her face.

The landing lights were on at Leeds when they touched down.

The driver was waiting for them. For the next hour and a half, Linda slept on one side of the Rolls with Sharon napping on the other.

Sharon awoke with the driver saying, "Madam," and shaking her shoulder. She opened her eyes to her grandmother's estate. There were lights in every window, automobiles parked all along the drive, and a sky speckled with stars. They climbed out of the back seat.

Their boots crunched over the gravel. Linda said, "Come on around the back. Mum often helps in the kitchen when your grandmother has one of her soirées."

Sharon followed Linda into the shadow alongside the house. A stone path led to the back. Light and the smell of food seeped out into the back garden. *I'm starved!*

Linda walked through the doorway. Sharon followed.

"Linda! What a grand surprise!" The woman behind the voice was a pound or two under one hundred and her silver hair was tied back into a tight bun. She wrapped her arms around Linda and held her cheek against Linda's neck.

"Hello, Anne," Linda said.

"Linda?" Honeysuckle carried a stacked tray of dirty dinner plates that she set down with a clatter on the counter. She too hugged Linda. "And you brought Sharon with you!"

"Mother, we need to talk," Linda said.

Sharon stopped, and all noise and motion in the room ceased while Linda led her mother outside.

Sharon hung her jacket on the back of a chair. "Where can I wash up?"

"Over there." Anne pointed to a sink on Sharon's left.

Sharon rolled up her sleeves. She scrubbed her hands and made a quick check in the mirror. *I look like an owl!* She worked at removing the oil and exhaust residue from her face.

Anne said, "Oi! Hand us one of the pies from the storeroom!"

Sharon looked at Anne, who was pointing at a closed door on the left-hand side of the kitchen. As she turned, she saw a pair of polished black shoes coming down the stairs into the kitchen.

She went to the storeroom door, opened it, and searched for a light switch. It was hidden inside a shelf just to her right. After she turned on the light, she looked around at the shelves of canned goods, jars, and sacks of food on either side of the narrow room. *There you are.* The pies were at the end of the room. She walked toward them and felt the cooler air touching the wet strands of hair framing her face.

The door closed.

The light went off.

Sharon turned.

There was the sound of leather-soled shoes on the stone floor.

"You're new here," a man's voice said.

"Who are you?" Sharon caught the scent of pipe smoke and gin.

"The man of the house." His hands touched her shoulders.

"What are you doing?" Sharon felt a knee jammed into her crotch. She tried to hit him, but he was too close.

He grabbed her wrists and held them together with one of his hands. With the other, he probed between her legs.

Sharon tried to breathe, but he had her pushed up against the shelves. "Don't. Please don't." Fear made it hard to think. *Just wait. When you get the chance, bite his ear off.*

The light flicked on.

Sharon looked to the open door. Honeysuckle stood there. Linda stood behind her.

"Marmaduke. I was hoping I would have the chance to introduce you to your niece," Honeysuckle said.

Marmaduke backed away from Sharon. "Very nice to finally meet you. Mother has told me that you were in England." He smiled and held out his hand.

Stunned, Sharon shook it. She saw that he had a hooked nose and slicked-back brown hair, and was wearing a black tuxedo with tails.

Marmaduke turned and waited for Honeysuckle to allow him out the door. "I'd best be returning to our guests."

Honeysuckle stepped into the room. Linda followed and closed the door.

Sharon could see that Honeysuckle had been crying.

"Are you all right, my dear?" Honeysuckle asked.

"I think so." Sharon tried to erase the memory of the crushing weight of him and found she could not.

Linda said, "Did he hurt you?"

Sharon shook her head and found that she was crying. "I was about to bite his ear off."

Honeysuckle's voice was a whisper. "When I realized you were inside and he was on the prowl, I rushed back in. I'm glad we were able to find you without too much delay."

"On the prowl? He's done this before?" Sharon asked.

Linda nodded. "He has quite a reputation for it, actually."

Sharon said, "What do I do?"

Honeysuckle put her hand on Sharon's cheek. "You do what we do in this type of circumstance."

"What's that?" Sharon asked.

Honeysuckle winked. "When the opportunity presents itself, you get even with the smarmy bastard! Now, let's get those pies Anne was asking for."

Linda opened the door and Sharon followed them into the kitchen.

"The guests are full of praise for the dinner." Cornelia stood at the top of the stairs leading to the main part of the house.

To Sharon, it looked like her grandmother was wrapped in green curtains and white lace.

"I'm so glad to see you and Linda here," Cornelia said to Sharon. "You must come and meet our guests."

Sharon looked at her clothing. "Perhaps another time." *Besides, I couldn't face Uncle Marmaduke at the moment.*

"Nonsense." Cornelia held out her hand.

Sharon nodded and found she was blushing. *Why do I feel ashamed?*

Cornelia waited for Sharon to climb the steps and take her hand. Sharon's grandmother led the way down a hallway into a great room where guests stood, drank, and chatted after dinner. The room was filled with tuxedos, evening dresses, tobacco smoke, and faces turned to inspect the young woman being led into the room by Cornelia Lacey.

Sharon was led to one corner where Marmaduke stood next to a blonde with pronounced cheekbones and startling blue eyes. She wore a black dress, white pearls, and black gloves that reached her elbows.

"This is your Aunt Cecilia," Cornelia said.

Cecilia held out her hand to Sharon. She squeezed Sharon's hand. "A very great pleasure." Cecilia's tone said the exact opposite.

Sharon pulled her hand away from the painful, pinching grip on the knuckle of her index finger.

"And this is your Uncle Marmaduke," Cornelia said.

Sharon looked at her uncle, remembering his hand between her legs. He offered his hand. She looked at it for a moment, then turned and walked out of the room, down the hallway, and into the kitchen.

It was well beyond midnight when Linda, Honeysuckle, and Sharon walked home.

"You're awfully quiet, Sharon." Honeysuckle held onto her daughter's arm.

"I have a lot to think about." Sharon was glad for the darkness.

"Are you crying?" Linda asked.

*Oh, shut up!* Sharon thought.

"Don't you dare feel as though you're somehow responsible for what Marmaduke did to you, my dear," Honeysuckle said.

o*At one thousand feet,* the Anson went into a right turn. Linda and Sharon sat one behind the other near the back door.

Sharon felt her emotions rising. They hit a pocket of rough air. The engines surged momentarily, then resumed their reassuring clatter.

"So what's troubling you?" Linda turned to face her friend.

"I traveled all this way in the middle of a war to find a family. It felt like I was half a person after my mother died. I thought that by coming here, I would feel like I belonged somewhere." Sharon studied her friend's face to see if she understood.

"It hasn't worked out the way that you'd hoped?"

"My uncle makes improper advances. My grandmother appears to be totally unaware of what her son is actually like. My father knows I exist, but doesn't know me at all."

"What were you expecting? Your mother traveled halfway around the earth to get away from her family, and she never returned."

Sharon opened her mouth to reply and closed it. *What do I say to that?*

"Nobody's family is perfect." Linda began to turn around.

"At least you've got a mother, a father, and a brother," Sharon said.

Linda shook her head. "But for how long? Hitler's ready to kick down the door and march across England like he did in France. We'll see how many of us survive the summer."

# CHAPTER 6

**Mother smiled as he said, "Here you go!"**

Linda held their chits high. Today she wore her uniform slacks, white blouse with rolled-up sleeves, and tie. She smiled broadly. "Finally!"

Sharon stuffed the crust of a mutton sandwich into her mouth and tried to smile despite her full cheeks.

"We're both going to Castle Bromwich. I've got a Spitfire!" Linda grabbed her friend around the waist and squeezed.

Sharon swallowed, choked, and coughed.

Linda released her hold and swatted Sharon on the back.

After the coughing subsided, Sharon wiped her eyes, picked up her kit, and followed Linda to the air taxi. This time it was a Dragon Rapide, with its elegant nose, dragonfly wings, and twin engines.

Fifty minutes later, when they were on finals for Castle Bromwich, Sharon saw the rows of factory roofs and all of the frenetic activity outside, where brand-new aircraft were lined up under a clear sky. *A perfect day.*

When they taxied to a stop, Linda was first outside the door.

Sharon had to wait in her seat as the pilot rushed past her, saying, "I've got to find some petrol."

By the time Sharon had collected her gear and exited the aircraft, Linda was already in the cockpit of a Spitfire, having the controls explained to her by a smiling mechanic.

Sharon pulled her chit out of a pocket and walked toward the dispersal hut.

A Merlin engine crackled to life.

Sharon looked over at Linda, who leaned left and right to see around the Spitfire's long nose. The engine began to smooth itself into a hum when Linda added power. She stood on one rudder, then the other, as she zigzagged her way along the taxiway while checking to make sure that no one was in front of her.

Sharon waited for the takeoff run so she'd be able to describe it for Linda later. She watched Linda dutifully do her run-up. She taxied onto the end of the runway, lined herself up into the wind, and applied throttle. The engine emitted a throaty hum. It began to roll forward; the tail lifted, then the wheels kissed the ground once before the wings carried the fighter into the air.

Sharon frowned when she spotted a line of black smoke trailing the Spitfire. The smoke was thicker and blacker than what usually passed for exhaust.

"Christ!" The mechanic waved his arms and went running after Linda's Spitfire. "Bail out!"

"She's too low!" someone else said.

Linda turned left when she realized her aircraft was on fire. She completed her turn and headed back toward them.

Sharon heard the bell of the fire tender. Another alarm sounded as the ambulance rushed to follow.

They saw the Spitfire turn onto finals with its wheels and flaps down. Flames licked along the belly of the aircraft.

"Christ, hurry!" the mechanic said.

Sharon started to run.

Linda flared for a landing. The propeller windmilled, causing smoke to boil over the wing roots.

With the limited visibility, she misjudged her height. The wheels hit the ground and the Spitfire bounced back into the air.

It dropped harder the second time. One undercarriage leg buckled, and the Spitfire started a ground loop as the lowered wingtip gouged the grass. The other undercarriage leg collapsed.

The propeller chewed into the ground. Dirt and grass flew into the air. The propeller blades curled back on themselves.

A wing bent up at the tip. The Spitfire slid along the grass and halted, with flames licking its nose and along the fuselage.

Linda pulled back the canopy.

The fire truck pulled up next to the wreck. Sharon saw a fireman running along a wing toward the cockpit, where the fire rose up on either side of him. The images of Linda and her rescuer's silhouette shivered in the heat. He reached inside, cut her safety harness, and hauled her out. He pushed her ahead of him as they ran back over the wing and away from the wreck.

Sharon grabbed at the pain under her ribs and gasped for air as she reached her friend.

Linda was pulling off her flying helmet.

Sharon looked down and saw that the fabric on the knees and shins of Linda's slacks hung in black tatters.

Sharon took a closer look at how pale Linda's face was.

Sharon looked at the front of Linda's legs. It wasn't just tattered black fabric hanging from her knees and shins — it was skin. Sharon inhaled the now-familiar stink of charred flesh.

Again, Sharon experienced the clarity of mind that she'd discovered while under attack by the Messerschmitt pilots.

She looked behind her and saw that the petrol bowser was next to the air taxi that brought them to Castle Bromwich. She spied the ambulance attendants pulling a stretcher out of the back of the ambulance.

Someone said, "We need tannic acid!"

"NO!"

Everyone, including Linda, turned toward Sharon.

"Put her on that stretcher!" Sharon pointed at the ambulance. "She's going on that aircraft!" She pointed at the Dragon Rapide. It had just finished refueling.

Everyone stood looking at her.

"NOW! She's being transported to the burn unit at East Grinstead! MOVE!"

It was later, when she had time to think, that she decided she had her father to thank for the voice she'd found.

By the time the ambulance pulled up next to the air taxi, the pilot was about to climb inside the aircraft.

He turned.

"There's a slight change in plans. The three of us —" Sharon pointed at Linda on the stretcher "— are going to East Grinstead."

"Where's your authorization?" the pilot asked.

Sharon lifted the blanket covering a shivering Linda. The lower half of both legs were blackened and blistered.

Sharon heard the pilot inhale. She knew he could smell the burned flesh. She took a breath and kept her voice low. "She's going into shock, and the hospital at East Grinstead treats burns. You're going to fly us there."

The pilot hesitated.

"Otherwise, these men" — she pointed at the ambulance driver and his assistant — "are prepared to restrain you, then help me load up my friend. I'll fly her to the hospital myself." Sharon prayed that no one would contradict her.

Linda moaned. The men unloaded the stretcher from the back of the ambulance and moved toward the Dragon Rapide.

"All right. Get her on board." The pilot turned, climbed onto the aircraft's wing, and entered through the side door. Sharon followed and helped manoeuver Linda inside.

The flight took too long. But then, five minutes would have been too long. *It's better than going by road,* Sharon thought. Linda's teeth were chattering by the time they were halfway there, and her body was shivering uncontrollably when they landed in a field near the hospital.

After the engines shut down, Sharon said, "Thank you," to the pilot who had radioed ahead to advise the hospital of their arrival. An ambulance was waiting, and the attendants helped her get a delirious Linda off the plane.

The younger of the two attendants said, "I suppose someone put tannic acid on her burns."

"There's no tannic acid on her burns! Just get her to the hospital," Sharon said.

The ride to the hospital was brief. A woman — who weighed more than two hundred pounds and wore a uniform that made her look like a nun — greeted them. "Women are not treated in this hospital!"

Sharon jumped down out of the back of the ambulance. "She's a pilot, she's badly burned, she's going into shock, and this is a hospital for burn victims!"

"No bloody whelp of a Yank is going to tell me how to run my hospital!" The nurse's entire face turned the colour of her rouged cheeks.

"It's okay, Margaret." A man put his arm around the nurse's shoulder.

"But Lewis, she's a girl," Margaret said.

Lewis turned Margaret around until they both faced Sharon. His head was turned to one side. A column of flesh connected his nose to his shoulder.

There was a sharp intake of breath. Sharon realized it was her.

Lewis' eyes smiled through a face being reconstructed after the fire. "How did you know to bring her here? Are we getting recommendations already?"

Sharon said, "I listened to a Lysander pilot. He'd been burned, and he said this was the hospital to come to."

Lewis said, "She's lucky. If you'd taken her anywhere else, they likely wouldn't have known what to do. We can make one exception, can't we, Margaret?"

"Make it quick, before I change my mind." Margaret looked around as if she expected someone in uniform to appear and contradict her.

Linda and the stretcher were carried down the hall behind Margaret, who issued orders and seemed to be pointing in all directions at once.

Sharon said, "By the way, I'm not a Yank. I'm a Canadian."

"Care for a walk?" Lewis asked.

Sharon looked at her hands. They hadn't stopped shaking since Linda was pulled from the wreck. She clasped them together, hoping to still them.

"She's a friend of yours?" Lewis asked.

Sharon nodded.

"You saw her burn?"

"Yes," Sharon said.

"I still smell my own burning skin when I'm having a nightmare."

He'd said it with such frank honesty that Sharon looked closer at his new face. The smile seemed permanent, and she saw that he had one ear. She said, "Her legs. They're black."

"That's what happens. The good news is they use salt baths here instead of that God-awful tannic acid, and they know how to prevent infection. Are you going to hang about? It could take a day or two before the doctors have anything to tell you. Does your friend have anyone else who would want to know she's here?"

Sharon stopped and looked around her at the stark, antiseptic hallways. "Oh, Christ! I need a telephone!"

"Come on, then." Lewis turned and walked down a hallway to the open door of a small office. He poked his head inside. "Quick, nobody's about. Make it fast, before Margaret shows up. In case you hadn't noticed, she's a stickler for regulations." He closed the door. Sharon sat down and tried to think of what to say. She dialed the number.

After five rings, Honeysuckle said, "Hello."

"Honeysuckle, it's Sharon."

"Oh, hello, dear." Honeysuckle hesitated. "There's something wrong, isn't there? What's happened to Linda?"

"She's in East Grinstead at the Queen Victoria Hospital. She was burned in a crash. We just arrived, and the doctors are with her," Sharon said.

"How badly is she burned, Sharon?" Honeysuckle asked.

*She sounds so calm.* "It's her legs. I don't how bad it is. All I know is that they treat burns here."

"When did the crash happen?" Honeysuckle asked.

"This morning," Sharon said.

"This morning! It's hardly midday. How did she get to a hospital so quickly?" Honeysuckle asked.

"She was flown here. What do you need me to do for you?"

Honeysuckle was quiet for a moment. "I have to make travel arrangements. Where did you say the hospital was?"

"East Grinstead. South of London on the A22."

"I'll leave shortly." Honeysuckle hung up.

# CHAPTER 7
[ AUGUST 1940 ]

**Mother looked tired when he said,** "Things are really heating up. The Hun is on the move. This delivery is a priority." He handed Sharon a chit. "We're short of pilots. You must know by now, the reward for good work is more work."

Sharon smiled, took the chit, and sprinted to catch the Anson air taxi. The pilot had already started one engine. She opened the door as he started the second engine.

"You're late! Where to?" the pilot said.

"Castle Bromwich." She sat in the only empty seat.

Spitfires were a priority, so she would be dropped off first.

In a matter of fifteen minutes, she was strapped in and starting the Merlin engine.

The fitter said, "This one's even got oxygen! You could squeeze in some high-altitude flying while no one is watching."

The propeller began to turn. The engine caught and belched black exhaust past the open cockpit. She caught a whiff of it and opened the throttle. The propeller blew the smoke away.

Sharon looked up at the cumulus clouds stacked between fifteen and twenty thousand feet. *Maybe today I will ignore the one-thousand-foot maximum.*

After the Spitfire kissed the runway for the last time and the wheels were tucked into the wings, she strapped on the oxygen mask. She set a compass heading for Biggin Hill and began to climb.

At ten thousand feet, she checked her course and made sure the oxygen was turned on. She leveled off at over twenty thousand feet, exhilarated by the climb. The aircraft felt nimble as she flew down a canyon between a pair of clouds. The canyon grew narrower and she squirted out the other side into clear air.

Ahead, another cloud. She flew over the hills and down into the valleys atop the cumulus cloud. The cloud whispered past as she dipped into an opaque world and out again. A bit of rough air made the Spitfire bounce.

A shadow flitted over a cloudy hill, then fell off the crest. Sharon felt her exhilaration shift to dread.

She looked up. A twin-engine fighter was diving on her. She recognized a Messerschmitt Bf 110 with a lethal combination of machine guns and cannons in its nose. Sharon pushed the stick hard right and steep-turned the Spitfire onto one wing.

The nose of the Nazi fighter sparkled as it opened fire. Tracer bullets streaked harmlessly by on Sharon's left. She continued her turn and watched the 110 duck into the cloud and then reappear. It was turning toward her, attempting to get into position to open fire again.

Sharon rolled the Spitfire onto its back and dove for a cloud. Inside the opaque middle of the grey, she was disoriented until the aircraft popped out the other side like a wet bar of soap.

The sky was filled with green twin-engined bombers flashing in and out of the shadows of the clouds. The Perspex noses glittered with reflected light. The wings of the bombers had black crosses and swastikas marking their tails. Exhaust trails left their dark pathways in the sky.

"Heinkels!" Sharon pushed the nose forward.

The engine coughed.

Sharon held her breath.

She aimed for a narrow opening between the lead bomber and the next Heinkel in formation.

The engine roared as fuel reentered the cylinders.

There were a series of images, each with its own momentary clarity. The face of a pilot. The head of a gunner. The green and grey of a camouflaged wing. A black cross outlined with white. The white tails of tracer bullets.

She ducked low into her seat, expecting the shock of a collision.

"Whoa!" She passed safely through the formation of bombers.

Sharon glanced in the rear-view mirror above her head. She saw the Messerschmitt BF 110 burst out of the cloud. Its pilot opened fire.

Tracer bullets reached out and passed over Sharon's Spitfire.

The 110 sliced the lead Heinkel in half. The bomber's wings and nose flew on for a moment, carried forward by momentum and its propellers. Then the stricken wreck pulled itself into a vertical stall.

The Messerschmitt, with one wing gone, promptly flipped onto its back and fell into another cloud.

Sharon dove through a cloud and found herself in a sky with two columns of smoke, some floating debris, and the blossom of a single parachute.

She continued the dive, changing direction every few seconds while maintaining a general heading toward Biggin Hill.

Fifteen minutes later, after a careful inspection of the sky, she landed and taxied over to the hangars. She switched off and was enveloped in the sudden silence.

Someone knocked on the Perspex. She saw the face of a mechanic on the other side and slid the canopy open.

"Must be hot up there — you're dripping." He helped her with the harness and oxygen mask.

Sharon took off her flying helmet and felt her hair. *He's right; I'm soaked with sweat.*

"Best be off and get yourself a cuppa," he said.

She stepped from the wing onto the ground.

She looked around her. A pair of mechanics worked on the engine of a Spitfire in the shade of the hangar.

Outside, a petrol bowser fueled another fighter.

There was the sound of an approaching aircraft. Sharon shaded her eyes to watch a Spitfire on finals and saw the pilot guide his aircraft to a slick landing. "It's like the battle never happened."

"What's that?" the mechanic asked.

"Oh, nothing." Sharon walked away in search of a cup of coffee.

She found one in a nearby tent and sat down outside in a chair. The sun caressed her face. She looked around to see if her father was nearby. She couldn't make up her mind if she wanted to see him or not. Their last meeting had not ended well, and it wouldn't be wise to tell him about her latest adventure.

A pilot walked toward the tent, and a group of men gathered around a table about ten feet away.

The approaching pilot said, "You boys missed an unbelievable bit of flying!"

The other pilots looked up expectantly.

"A lone Spit just broke up a formation of Heinkels! He dove out of a cloud with a Messerschmitt 110 on his tail. The Spitfire flew right between the two lead bombers, and the Messerschmitt opened fire. The Jerry pilot in the 110 mustn't have been paying attention, because he flew right into the lead Heinkel. The rest of the bombers ended up in a bloody shambles. I fell into the middle of them all and managed to pick off two."

"Any idea who the other pilot was?" one of the sergeant pilots asked.

"He landed just before me. Must be around here somewhere." The pilot looked around. "Who just arrived?"

The pilots all looked at Sharon.

A pilot said, "That young girl over there, the one with the brown hair, she landed just before you did."

One of the pilots leaned forward in his chair. "Couldn't have been her. The pilot must have landed somewhere else."

Sharon stood up and walked away. "Maybe the air taxi is here." *Couldn't have been her! You arrogant pricks!* She felt her body vibrate with anger.

As she passed the mouth of a hangar, a voice said, "I hear the female pilots are getting four extra days off every month. It seems they're unable to fly because of the curse."

Sharon turned and saw Bloggs in the shade next to the hangar. There were other men with him, smoking.

One of them laughed.

"What did you say?" Sharon walked toward them. *You superior bastards!*

Two of the men laughed and prodded Bloggs. His face turned red.

"I asked you a question!" Sharon stopped less than a yard from Bloggs.

Bloggs took a step back.

"Well?" *Stop baiting him!*

He moved a bit to her right.

Sharon's hands made fists. "Having trouble dealing with a woman who's not afraid of you?"

Bloggs turned to the men, who were laughing at him. One held his arm up to point at Sharon, then dropped it limply to his side.

"Hey, you lot!" the voice came from behind Sharon.

The men stopped laughing and dropped their cigarettes.

Sharon turned to face her father.

"The war's not waiting on you boys. We've got a new Spitfire that needs guns and ammunition. We're short of aircraft after that shambles this morning!" Patrick had his shirtsleeves rolled up and his fists on his hips. "And you!" He pointed at Bloggs. "Is that any way to talk to a young lady?"

Bloggs smirked. "She's far from being a lady."

"You smarmy bastard, she's my daughter!" Patrick cocked his arms, made fists and moved closer to Bloggs.

Sharon had never felt a combination of pride at being her father's daughter and fear that he was about to beat Bloggs to a bloody pulp.

Mechanics appeared from inside the hangar to join the smokers. "Oi!"

"What's got your wind up?" a mechanic asked.

Several of the men got in between Patrick and Bloggs.

One said, "Sergeant Major! He's just another posh bastard with a pair of wings!"

Bloggs backed up a few steps, then retreated down the side of the hangar.

The mechanics studied Sharon with renewed interest.

"Should've known!" one said.

"What's that mean, Nigel?" Patrick asked.

"I heard the pilots talkin' over there." Nigel pointed toward the canteen. "They said a pilot broke up a bomber formation, and at least two Jerries went down. They thought she couldn't have done it, but if she's your daughter, that would make it entirely possible." Nigel pushed his shoulders back, waiting for Patrick to do his worst.

Patrick turned to Sharon. "You flew through a Nazi formation?"

Sharon nodded.

Patrick put his hand to his forehead. "Christ!"

"It's not like I went looking for trouble," Sharon said.

"But trouble sure has a way of finding you!" Patrick pointed at his men. "Get that new Spitfire fitted out. We'll need it to be ready to go as soon as possible."

The crew wended its way into the hangar.

"I'd better go and get a ride back to White Waltham," Sharon said.

"That might be a bit of a problem." He walked alongside her.

She breathed in the scent of him under the oil and the shaving cream.

The pilot of the air taxi was asleep under the wing of the Anson.

"Drunken bastard," Patrick said.

Sharon saw Roger on his back with an arm draped over his eyes. He was snoring. "Dad, can you give me a hand?"

The word was out before she could think about it. It hung there for a minute.

"Yes." Patrick's voice broke. He put his hand over his mouth and pretended to cough.

They picked up the snoring Roger and hefted him in through the back door of the aircraft.

Patrick said, "Christ, he smells like the backside of a pub. He landed about an hour ago. The landing was bloody awful. He stumbled out, started drinking from a flask, and passed out."

"Just another hazard of my present occupation," Sharon said.

Patrick laughed. "You're not going to let him fly, are you?"

"Hell no! Help me strap him into a seat, and I'll fly us both back to White Waltham." Sharon climbed inside the aircraft. It smelled of fabric, oil, sweat, and gin.

She lifted Roger under the arms. Patrick grabbed him by the knees. They crammed him into his seat.

Patrick tightened the harness. "Don't want him getting up and moving about. Want me to get some rope?"

"He'll be fine, I think." She turned to her father. "Thank you."

"My pleasure." He took her hand. "The next time you're here, there are things we need to talk about."

"What things?" Sharon asked.

Patrick released her hand and squeezed his way down the fuselage, stepped out the door, and poked his head back in. "Next time."

He closed the door.

# CHAPTER 8

**"You look better."** Sharon sat down on a metal chair in Linda's hospital room. "I brought you some magazines." She lifted the cloth bag and put it on the table next to Linda's bed.

"Honeysuckle wants to see you." Linda closed her eyes, opened them, breathed into her hand to check her breath, and grimaced.

"What about?" Sharon asked.

"I'm not really sure. You know my mother — she can be a bit secretive."

"Not with me." Sharon shook her head.

"Did I tell you Honeysuckle wants to talk with you?"

"Yes." Sharon nodded.

"Oh. Didn't I just say that? I'm a little fuzzy. The morphine, you know. Wonderful stuff, by the way."

"So the doctors are putting your ass on your legs?"

"You have such a blunt way of explaining the most delicate and intricate of surgeries. And, as usual, you've hit the nail right on the head. You always manage to cheer me up with that direct approach to any problem." Linda smiled.

"You were saying that your mother wants to see me?" *God, Linda looks so thin and her hair has lost its shine.*

"Yes, she said that you must drop by when you get a delivery close to her neck of the woods." Linda looked out the window as a man walked past.

"What do you see?"

"One of the boys who's had his nose burned off. They're building him a new one. You must have seen one or two on your way in. They have their new noses connected to one shoulder. Quite a shocker when you first see it. Now it's all old hat. They're still worried I might lose a leg, you know." Linda looked at her friend.

"I didn't know."

"And they say you're the reason why I have any hope at all of keeping both. How did you know to bring me here?"

"The pilot we met the morning your brother flew in from France. Remember?"

"Vaguely." Linda stared at the wall. "If memory serves, I was busy beating him up."

"Richard, the Lysander pilot, had been burned. He told me about this hospital."

"Guinea pigs."

"What?" Sharon asked.

"The boys call themselves guinea pigs. Much of the medicine practiced here is experimental. Sometimes it's called plastic surgery."

"Plastic. Sounds like something new." Sharon looked at the mini-tent of elevated white sheet above Linda's legs.

"Speaking of new, what's new with your father?" Linda asked.

"I saw him again. Just after I flew through a Luftwaffe bomber formation."

Linda sat up on her elbows. "Come on, tell me how you managed to find yourself doing something that mad!"

Sharon told Linda about flying into cloud, being hunted by a Messerschmitt Bf 110, and the ensuing collision.

"I don't know all of the rules about air combat, but I think you may be well on your way to being an ace. That makes three, if memory serves." Linda raised her eyebrows. "You Canadians are such a fierce lot."

Sharon shrugged. "It was all about staying alive, believe me. It was plain dumb luck that I missed colliding with one of the Heinkels."

Linda shook her head. "It was more than luck. Every time we fly together, I'm quite envious of your instinctive ability to react to different circumstances."

"Too bad I'm such a disaster when it comes to having a family."

"Look, your mother left to get you away from that brother and father of hers. Honeysuckle said your mother was so different from everyone else in her family. She wasn't pompous and posh like the men. And she didn't pretend everything was just fine in her family, like Cornelia does. Everyone seems to think that your mother was really quite remarkable." Linda reached for a glass of water. "Christ, I'm always so thirsty in this place."

"I miss her every day."

Linda looked over top of the glass. "Of course you do. Just don't miss what's right in front of your face."

"What does that mean?"

"It means that a family isn't always made up of blood relations. If you can't see that, then you may have the eyesight of an ace, but you're still blind as a bat." Linda sat the glass down next to her bed. "My arse is sore. I'm going to roll over on my side."

o *"Tempsford? Where's that, Mother?"* Sharon asked.

Mother scratched his head. "Not sure, exactly. Apparently, it's near Bedford. Once they drop you off at the assembly hangar for the Lysander, someone will surely give you directions." He handed her a chit and pointed her in the direction of the duty Anson that was to drop her at her next delivery.

"I'm sorry, Mother, but where's Bedford?"

"North of London, near Cambridge."

She was the first to be dropped off at a small airfield west of London where Lysanders were assembled.

An aircraftsman leaned against the open hangar door. "You the one here to pick up the Lysander?"

"That's me." Sharon felt the morning sun against the back of her neck. *It might turn out to be a rare day for flying.*

The aircraftsman reached into his shirt pocket and pulled out an envelope. "I was told to give you this."

Sharon took the envelope and opened it. Inside was a detailed map placing Tempsford about halfway between Bedford and Cambridge. A compass heading was written across the top of the map.

After she completed the walk around, Sharon could sense the eyes of the aircraftsman on her back as she made the ten-foot climb up the side of the Lysander and into the cockpit.

She kept her ATA handbook of aircraft tucked into the pocket of her coveralls as she went though her checks. She said, "Clear!" and started the engine. The airframe shuddered. The exhaust belched smoke. She waited for the engine to even out, then began to roll ahead.

After running up the engine and completing her preflight checks, she aimed the Lysander into the wind and marveled as its high, long wings bit into the wind and carried her into the air after a remarkably short takeoff run.

The expanse of Plexiglas made the cockpit into a greenhouse. Sharon wiped the sweat from her forehead as she leveled off at one thousand feet and headed north. She opened a side window to get some air moving inside the cockpit.

After about twenty minutes, she thought, *I've got the feel of this thing*. She tapped the envelope in her breast pocket and played the directions back in her mind as she maintained her heading and looked ahead for Bedford. The Lysander's high wing made it easy to see what was beneath her.

For a few minutes, she almost enjoyed England as the landscape rolled along. It was relatively easy to find Bedford, even though she'd never been there before, and then she headed east.

Tempsford was only seven miles away. She spotted the runway, checked the wind, and was the only aircraft in the circuit. She landed on the grass strip and taxied toward a collection of construction equipment. A man with a leather vest waved his arms over his head, then pointed to his left.

She taxied toward a patch of tarmac, gave the Lysander's Bristol engine a twitch of throttle, kicked the rudder, and swung the aircraft around. Sharon shut down, undid her harness, slid the canopy open, and climbed over the side.

"It's good to see you again."

Sharon turned as she pulled off her leather flight helmet. Standing there was Michael — Linda's brother. His hair was a sandy blond in the morning sunlight, and he was a head taller than her.

She felt uncomfortable under the scrutiny of his blue eyes. "What are you doing here?" Sharon pushed her brown hair back, combing it with the fingers of her right hand. *I must look a sight.*

"I've been awaiting your arrival, actually." Michael nodded in the direction of a black, silver-grilled Austin parked at the edge of the tarmac.

Sharon frowned and looked sideways at him. "What do you mean?" *Was my being here part of a plan? Why am I so nervous?*

"I mean, I wanted to thank you for taking care of Linda, and I wanted to ask you some questions."

"Why?" Sharon looked around her. Construction workers were pouring tea from flasks and leaning against the back of a truck.

"Honeysuckle told me to bring some coffee and a bite to eat. It's in the trunk of the Austin." He turned and walked toward the car.

Sharon waited for a moment, then followed. *He obviously went to a great deal of trouble. How did he know it would be me doing the delivery?*

When she approached the car, Sharon heard a snarl. "What's that?"

Michael opened the boot and pulled out a picnic basket. "What's what?"

This time, she heard a growl.

"Are there bears around here?" Sharon asked.

"Bears?" Michael began to laugh. "It's my mother — she's snoring!"

"Honeysuckle is here?" Sharon asked.

"What? Who's there?" The voice came from inside the car.

Sharon leaned in an open window. The car smelled of oil and leather.

Honeysuckle was in the back seat. She wiped her mouth. "There you are!"

Sharon stepped back.

Honeysuckle opened the door, stood up, and hugged Sharon close. "You darling!"

Sharon looked at Michael and asked, "What did I do?"

"You made sure that Linda was flown to the hospital." Michael set the picnic basket on the grass.

"The surgeon thinks he'll be able to save her legs because of you." Honeysuckle wiped at her eyes. "If you hadn't done that, she might have died from shock or infection. They use salt baths to treat burns at East Grinstead and have a very high survival rate for burn patients." Honeysuckle pulled out a handkerchief and gave her face a working over.

"Should we eat?" Michael asked.

Both women glared at him.

Honeysuckle said, "Men think only of their stomachs."

"It was just a question!" He picked up the basket and headed for the shade under the wing of the Lysander.

Honeysuckle took Sharon by the elbow, and they followed Michael. "I hope you don't mind. I made Harry set this up. They needed aircraft delivered here. It's a new airfield. All very secretive, you know. I simply wanted to thank you face to face."

Sharon shrugged. "I just did what needed to be done."

"That's exactly why we're here." Michael set the basket down in the shade.

Honeysuckle released Sharon and pulled the red-and-white checked cloth off the top of the basket. "What have we here?"

"You packed it, Mother," Michael said.

"Where's your sense of humour? You've become so serious since you returned from France." Honeysuckle pulled out sandwiches wrapped in waxed paper. She handed the first to Sharon. "It's real ham, not that disgusting stuff from a can."

Sharon sat down next to Honeysuckle. For a moment, Sharon imagined she caught the scent of her mother. She closed her eyes, trying to hold onto a rich memory of Leslie's hand on hers. It was gone. She opened the waxed paper and inhaled the scent of fresh-baked bread, butter, mustard, and ham. Sharon longed for home as she bit into the sandwich.

Michael sat down next to her. His arm brushed against hers.

Sharon felt a tingling in her belly.

Michael reached across and took the Thermos.

Sharon felt heat on her face.

He poured a cup of coffee and handed it to her.

"Thanks." Sharon held the sandwich in one hand and the coffee in the other.

Honeysuckle looked over as the workmen started up some of the machinery. "What are they doing?"

Michael ignored his mother's question and turned to Sharon. "So, being from Canada may mean that you speak French."

"Don't you dare change the subject, Michael, and don't even think about recruiting Sharon for your bloody nighttime flights into France! It's dangerous enough being in England!" Honeysuckle pointed a finger at her son, then turned to Sharon. "Linda told me about your close shave with those Messerschmitts."

*I hope she didn't tell you all of it.*

Michael frowned at Honeysuckle.

"I was just making conversation, Mother." Michael handed her a cup of coffee.

"You forget, I know how you and your father work. There will be no recruiting of Sharon. Is that understood? We will not repay her kindness to Linda by putting her in more danger."

Michael went to reply.

Honeysuckle held up her hand to stop him.

Michael took a bite of sandwich instead.

*What is going on here?* Sharon thought.

"Michael and his father are beginning the organizing and supplying of resistance forces inside occupied France." Honeysuckle looked at Michael, as if daring him to tell her to be quiet. "They need pilots to fly our people in and out of the continent. If you spoke French, he would then try to recruit you. He may, in fact, be trying to recruit you anyway. You have quite a reputation in the RAF. The Royal Air Force is such a closed little community, you know." She looked at Sharon. "Yes, I said RAF, not ATA. You see, I have many sources of information, just like my husband."

*Damn it, Linda, your devotion to revealing secrets can be so annoying.*

"And no, Linda did not tell me about the way you broke up that Nazi bomber formation," Honeysuckle said.

"Mother, all of this is supposed to a secret! By rights, I should have you arrested." Michael smiled at Sharon.

Honeysuckle waved her sandwich at him dismissively. "Sharon's one Canadian who is not going to be used as cannon fodder to protect the Empire! Now, we need to talk about your Uncle Marmaduke."

"My uncle?" Sharon asked.

"Yes, your uncle. He's certainly no relation to me, although he has tried to have relations," Honeysuckle said.

"Mother!" Michael shook his head. "What's come over you?"

"Well, he has a way of making his presence known to all of the young women who live near the Lacey Estate. And he thinks that you" — Honeysuckle pointed at Sharon — "have come to England with the sole intention of laying claim to your mother's property."

"What?" Sharon asked. *What kind of mess am I in now?*

"Marmaduke treats his servants as if they don't exist. So when he talks with his wife or his mother, he often talks in front of the people under his mother's employ. And they talk with me." Honeysuckle looked at her son as though expecting him to contradict her.

"That's not why I came to England," Sharon said.

"Yes, we know that, but your uncle is a man who thinks that everyone else in the world was meant to provide for people like him. He believes that rules are meant for others to follow, and that he has the right to live his life the way he does because of who he is. Most of all, he is not a man to be taken lightly. It would be better if you were careful in your dealings with him. And it could be a disaster if you were unaware of his motivations." Honeysuckle reached for her coffee.

"It's true, Marmaduke has become comfortable in his role as a member of the privileged class," Michael said. "And he has been known to take certain liberties. At the same time, certain events from the Lacey family's past mean that he must navigate some very treacherous territory."

"We both know that," Honeysuckle said.

Sharon waited. *What are they talking about? I'm inside the conversation, but outside of their understanding.*

"His desire to conceal certain embarrassing family secrets could become useful," Michael said.

"This is such a dirty business," Sharon said. *My uncle comes close to raping me, and all we can do is politely dance around it by saying things like "embarrassing family secrets."*

Michael said, "We're at war. It's all about dirty secrets and dirty tricks."

*Enough of this!* Sharon finished her sandwich and rolled the waxed paper into a ball. Above her, a pair of blackbirds with orange bills dove, climbed, and turned. The pair swooped low over Sharon's head and disappeared behind a shrub. She stood up, finished the last of her coffee, and looked down at Honeysuckle. "Please tell me what my mother was like when she was young."

"I've been hoping you would ask." Honeysuckle stood and brushed off her dress. "Come on, Michael, you drive us to Bedford. Sharon and I have things to talk about." She reached into the picnic basket and pulled out a packet of letters tied together with a while ribbon. "Your mother wrote these to me. Would you like them? I've been saving them for you."

# CHAPTER 9

**Sharon put her uniform jacket** on the back of the chair at the cottage. *Will I ever see Linda back here, stuffing her face with fish and chips?*

She turned back to the door and saw a letter leaning up against the baseboard. It had been pushed through the mail slot.

Sharon bent over, scooped the letter up, and read the return address. The name Patrick O'Malley was written in the top corner. She sat down and used her nails to peel back the envelope flap. Her thumb and forefinger picked out the letter and unfolded it. Possibilities ran through her mind, then she began to read.

> DEAR SHARON,
>
> I'VE BEEN WRITING THIS LETTER FOR A FORTNIGHT.
>
> YOU HAVE A BROTHER. THERE, I'VE SAID IT. A HALF-BROTHER. BUT THERE'S NOTHING HALFWAY ABOUT SEAN.
>
> I'D LIKE YOU TWO TO MEET. PERHAPS YOU COULD GET A DELIVERY TO BIGGIN HILL FOR AUGUST 18TH? IT'S HIS ELEVENTH BIRTHDAY, AND I THINK IT WOULD BE A GOOD TIME FOR THE TWO OF YOU TO MEET.
>
> YOUR FATHER,
> PATRICK

Sharon read the letter again. *I have a brother.* She closed her eyes and savoured the euphoria.

# CHAPTER 10

**"I'll do what I can."** Mother had dark circles under his grey eyes, and he leaned with one elbow on the counter at the White Waltham dispersal hut. He handed her the chit with her delivery. "It's another Lysander, same place as last time. Cloak and dagger stuff." He winked.

"I wonder what he wants this time?" Sharon looked at the chit and its very specific directions. *How come I'm so nervous?*

"You know, if it's possible, I will get you a Spitfire delivery on the 18th."

Sharon smiled. "I know you will. It's just. . ."

"There's a bloody war on," Mother said.

"Exactly. Mother? Do you know what an eleven-year-old boy would want for his birthday?"

"Now you've asked a difficult question. Give me a day or two to think. Best be on your way. More and more talk of Hitler's invasion fleet and Goering's Luftwaffe gathering itself for a big push."

Sharon picked up her gear and her chit and made her way to the Anson waiting at the edge of the airfield. A handful of pilots stood leaning on the wings or smoking cigarettes a polite distance from the aircraft.

*Thank God, the pilot isn't Jolly Roger the drunken sod. Christ! I'm beginning to sound like I was born here.*

The pilot was fiftyish and looked more like a farmer in his baggy grey flight suit. "Alright, you lot. Grab your kit. Lots of deliveries this morning. Can't let Herr bloody Hitler and his boys march right in and take over, now can we?"

"Being a bit optimistic again, Douglas?" One of the pilots was busy crushing a cigarette under his boot.

Douglas smiled and studied the passengers from under two thickets that passed for eyebrows. "Have we been invaded yet?"

The pilot heaved his parachute onto his shoulder. "Not so far."

"Then we've got work to do." Douglas squeezed himself inside the aircraft and the rest followed. He settled himself into the pilot's seat and looked at his clipboard. "Which one of you lot is Lacey?"

"Me." Sharon raised her hand, then dropped it. The other pilots smirked at her unintentional impression of a schoolgirl.

"We're not in bloody school," someone said.

"Asshole," Sharon said.

"Another Yank who doesn't know her place," someone else said.

"I'm not a Yank!" Sharon hated the way they'd managed to put her on the defensive.

"Save your fight for the Germans." Douglas looked at Sharon. "Sit near the door — we're dropping you off first."

She did as she was told. After they were in the air, she thought, *Douglas looks like a labourer, but he's a brilliant pilot.*

Thirty minutes later, she was watching the Anson take off. She walked over to a hangar where a Lysander stood waiting.

A mechanic held his hand out, and she gave him the chit. He stuffed one hand in his pocket. The other held the chit at arm's length. He was shorter than Sharon, and she could see flakes of dandruff along the part of his black hair.

"Give us a hand," he said as he turned toward the Lysander. These were the only words he spoke.

Twenty minutes later, she was flying through a grey sky with a heading that would take her to Tempsford.

More than once, she thought, *I wonder if Michael will be there.*

There was no sign of him or his black automobile as she touched down, then taxied over to the framed skeleton of a hangar that hadn't been there the last time she'd flown in.

The engine was ticking as it cooled when she climbed out of the Lysander.

"Welcome to Gibraltar Farm. A pleasant flight, I hope." Michael stood under a tree, holding a flask. "I brought coffee this time, but no lunch, I'm afraid. Could I give you a lift to Bedford?"

Sharon hefted her parachute and found herself smiling. "A ride would be nice. I thought this was called Tempsford."

"Only to those in the know. Gibraltar Farm is the cover name. Come on. The car is over here."

She followed him to a barn. "Let me guess. Gibraltar Barn?"

Michael turned and smiled. "Of course."

Around the back of the barn was a red two-seat MG TB Roadster.

He opened the passenger door for her after she stowed her parachute behind the seat.

He climbed in the other side and poured her a coffee from the Thermos. "I hope it's still warm."

Sharon took the cup. "What's happened?"

Michael smacked the stopper into the neck of the Thermos. "I should have expected you to get right to the point."

Sharon sipped her coffee.

He started the engine. "More than one thing, actually."

"Who sent you this time?" Sharon watched his reaction.

She hung on with one hand, balancing her coffee out over her knees with the other. The MG bumped over the grass until they reached a gravel road rutted by the passage of heavy trucks.

"My mother wanted you to know that Linda's legs are beginning to heal quite nicely." He turned onto a tarmac road.

"I'm sorry I haven't been back to see her." Sharon took a careful sip of coffee.

Michael shook his head. "I haven't, either. It appears that the war is entering a crucial stage. We know that the Luftwaffe is preparing for air raids aimed at destroying the RAF and its airfields. The same tactics were used in Europe: destroy the air forces of countries like

Poland and France, then send in the tanks and troops. The tactics have been very successful up until now."

"What do you mean 'until now'?"

Michael eased into a turn.

Sharon leaned into him. *He smells so good, but he's Linda's brother!*

"The Channel. The Navy. The RAF. I think the Nazis are over-confident, and we have nothing to lose. It's a very unpredictable combination." Michael shifted into top gear as the road opened up in front of them.

"You think the Nazis won't invade?" Sharon asked.

"I think an invasion will depend on first destroying the RAF, and then the Royal Navy. And I think for the next month or so, you will be very busy, as the Luftwaffe begins its attacks in earnest. I wanted to warn you to be careful." He glanced at her.

"You said there was more than one thing."

"Your uncle has decided that Cornelia needs a new will."

Sharon shrugged. "So?"

"Marmaduke has been embarrassed. He made improper advances toward his sister's daughter. In his mind, you're responsible for that embarrassment, and now he wants to make sure that you'll be unable to inherit any of the estate left by Cornelia. In fact, he's put the wheels in motion by visiting the family lawyer." Michael downshifted behind a truck that was moving slowly and taking up more than half the road.

Sharon shook her head. "How have I become the villain in this? And how do you know so much?"

"My mother knows the lawyer's secretary. You must understand that the entire district lived under the tyranny of your grandfather. An information-gathering network exists so that local people have an early warning system. It was excellent training for my present occupation. As far as you being the villain, it's an old tactic used by your uncle and grandfather. They bully, and then play the victim when they're caught. After that, they usually resort to character assassination aimed at destroying confidence in the people who confront them." Michael eased right to see around the truck, then ducked back when he saw a motorcar approaching.

"What if I'm planning to return to Canada and want nothing more to do with Uncle Marmaduke?"

Michael smiled at her. "We expected you might feel that way. The problem is that my mother sees the situation in another light entirely. She's decided that it's her duty to defend you. She really is tenacious, you know."

"The Germans really don't have a chance against people like you."

"And your uncle has no chance against my mother."

"How is that?"

"She knows who killed your grandfather." Michael downshifted, accelerated, and passed the truck.

"I thought he died of natural causes."

"That's what everyone was intended to think." Michael eased back onto the left side of the road.

# CHAPTER 11

**"There's a gentleman waiting for you in the dispersal hut."**
Mother passed her on the way to the hangar.

"Is he wearing a suit and carrying a briefcase?" Sharon asked.

"As a matter of fact, he is," Mother said over his shoulder.

*Michael was right. Uncle Marmaduke has sent someone.* Sharon carried her goggles and flight helmet with one hand and unzipped her flight suit with the other. The sun dropped its ample belly over the western horizon. She opened the door to the dispersal hut.

The man was wearing a tweedy brown three-piece suit and had unruly salt-and-pepper hair, and a pair of equally unkempt eyebrows.

He held a briefcase in his lap as he sat on a wooden chair and appraised her arrival. "Miss Sharon Lacey."

"That's correct." Sharon took a chair across the table from him and leaned her back up against the wall. She watched him warily.

"My name is Walter McGregor. I represent Marmaduke Lacey, your mother's brother."

"In what capacity?" Sharon rubbed her face. *God, I need some sleep.*

"The family solicitor. My father and I have represented your family for more than fifty years." Walter reached inside his briefcase and removed a manila file.

"My family? Somehow I don't think dear Uncle Marmaduke would include me as a family member." She looked out the window at the setting sun and wondered at the richness of the greens.

"Quite perceptive of you. And may I say, you bear a very close resemblance to your mother. A lovely person. We were very sad to see her leave the country. Her personality was nothing at all like that of her father or brother."

"So I've heard." *How come I'm not nervous? Just a few weeks ago, my stomach would have been in knots.*

Walter put several pieces of official-looking paper on the table. "Marmaduke Lacey has asked me to have you sign these documents."

"What kinds of documents are they?" *Go ahead. I'll play dumb for the moment.*

"Your uncle wants you to give up any and all claims to property held in the Lacey family name."

Sharon heard the change in tone when Walter said the words "your uncle." She waited.

"May I ask what you do?" Walter asked.

"I'm a pilot in the ATA."

"The Air Transport Auxiliary?"

"That's correct." *Where's he headed with this?*

"My sons have signed up. One in the Royal Air Force. The other is in the Navy." Walter tapped his fingers on the documents.

"I hope your sons are safe."

Walter stared at her. "That's exactly the kind of thing your mother would have said. And it's precisely what your uncle didn't ask me the last time we talked."

"You knew my mother well?"

Walter nodded. "Yes, and I liked her very much. We spent some years together in school."

Sharon leaned forward to look at the documents. *So, Mom, how many beaux did you have?*

"As I've said, we've represented the Lacey family for some time, and since you're a member of said family, I feel I must advise you not to sign away your rights. I did tell your uncle that I would present these documents to you." Walter reached for the papers and put them back inside the folder. "I would feel comfortable reporting to him that you respectfully declined to sign."

Sharon frowned. "Why come all this way, then?"

"To find out if it was true that Leslie's daughter had returned. And now I find that you've come halfway around the world at considerable risk. And I'm assuming that flying for the ATA must involve some risk?"

*You have no idea.* "You heard what happened to Linda Townsend?"

"Yes, and I've heard that thanks to you, she is recovering." Walter stood and put the folder in his briefcase. "You're putting yourself in harm's way. My sons are doing the same. All while Marmaduke Lacey sits warm and safe in a country home and has the temerity to think that I would quietly allow you to sign away your inheritance. He really doesn't know me very well at all. I was a friend of your mother's."

Sharon stood.

Walter offered his hand, and she shook it.

He said, "If you require any legal advice, I would be proud to represent you." He handed her his business card and left.

# CHAPTER 12

**"The next set of skin grafts is tomorrow."** Linda sat propped up in her bed. Her red hair had grown and she had it tied at the back. She'd taken the time to apply lipstick. She glanced at the ceiling.

Sharon thought, *What do I say to her?* "How many grafts will it take?"

"I don't know. This could go on for months. Years, perhaps." She took a long breath. "The nurse said I could go outside. I have to keep my legs covered. What do you think? Do you want to wheel me around East Grinstead for an hour or two?"

Five minutes later, after the nurse helped them find a wheelchair, Sharon was pushing Linda down the hall.

"Oi! You cheeky bastard!"

Sharon looked left through a doorway. She caught a glimpse of two young men sitting across from one another. One held cards fanned by a hand with stumps rather than fingers. A column of flesh joined his nose to his shoulder. The other had a nose, no ears, and a relief-map face of scar tissue.

She continued down the hall.

"Left," Linda said.

They passed a keg propped on a table in the corner.

"Is that beer?" Sharon asked.

"That's right. The rules around here are simple. You can do what you like, as long as it doesn't harm anyone else. That way!" Linda pointed.

Sharon backed out through the doorway and into the sunlight.

Linda closed her eyes. "That feels wonderful."

"Where are we going?"

Linda pointed to the left. "The Guinea Pig Pub, of course."

The pub was on a corner in amongst rows of houses and businesses.

Sharon stopped in front of a narrow doorway. "How will I get you through there?"

"Wait a minute."

"For what?"

There was a tapping from inside the window.

The door opened.

One man was in RAF blue. He had neither eyebrows nor ears and was in the process of having his face rebuilt. The other wore an apron and had arms the size of hams. He leaned over. Linda wrapped her arms around his neck, and he lifted her. "Park the chair against the wall," he said to Sharon.

Sharon did as she was told. The scarred man held the door open to allow her to follow them into the pub. Her eyes smarted at the smoke.

Linda was sitting at a table with a group of young men dressed in a variety of styles, including white hospital gowns and an unofficial mismatch of blue RAF uniforms.

"What's your poison?" asked the barman with the massive arms. "Call me Robert."

"She'll have what I'm having." Linda raised a pint and winked at Sharon. "Come on, there's a spot right here." She pulled out the empty chair next to her.

Linda went around the table. "Willy, Ginger, Pat, and Richard." Each of the men nodded or smiled as he was introduced.

Willy wore a patch over his eye. He was the only one of them who had a full head of hair. It hung to the right, leaving a bald patch over his left ear. He pointed at his eyepatch. "Lost my glass one. If you find it, please hand it over."

"Of course." *The wig looks ridiculous, yet no one seems to notice,* Sharon thought.

Robert put a pint in front of her. "One of Linda's ATA friends, are you?"

"That's right." Sharon nodded.

"We hear you've got three Jerries to your credit," Ginger said.

Sharon looked at Linda, who was smiling behind her pint. "We do some chatting in the pub. I was telling the truth, so don't get all upset with me. It's just pilot talk."

Sharon shook her head and reached for her drink. As she lifted the glass, she thought, *It got awfully quiet in here.*

She looked over her glass and saw four and a half pairs of eyes on her. She tipped the glass and heard something clink at the bottom.

Willy smiled.

Sharon began to drink.

"Bottoms up!" Willy said.

"Cheers!" Ginger said.

Intuition provided Sharon with the most likely answer to their odd behaviour. She continued to drink deeply, slowing as she reached the bottom of the glass and hesitating for effect. She put her glass down, then reached inside her mouth.

"Find something?" Willy asked.

Sharon pulled out a glass orb, reached across the table, and dropped it into Willy's glass. "Ever have a prairie oyster?"

Willy asked, "Prairie what?"

She reached over, lifted his eyepatch, and stared into his other good eye. She pulled the patch back and then let it snap back against Willy's forehead.

"Ouch!" Willy rubbed his head.

Laughter erupted in the pub.

Sharon leaned back in her chair. The laughter ebbed. "When calves are branded in the spring, the young bulls are castrated. The testicles are kept and cooked with butter and onions in a frying pan. Quite tasty, actually. They're called prairie oysters."

Robert thumped Sharon on the back and put another pint in front of her. "Finally! Someone's got the best of Willy!"

Linda winked at Sharon.

Ginger pounded the table with a fingerless hand.

Pat threw his head back and laughed some more.

Richard reached over and pulled Willy's wig off. "Now you're entirely exposed!"

An hour later, after Linda had been poured into the wheelchair, Sharon pushed from behind, using the chair for support.

"What are your intentions as far as Michael's concerned?" Linda asked.

"What?" *Where did that come from? He's your brother, he's handsome, and I don't know how I feel when I'm around him. Although I do look forward to seeing him again.*

"I'm the last person you should play coy with. I owe you my life — well, at least my legs. And you owe me the truth."

"I have no idea what you're talking about."

"Michael's absolutely gaga over you. You can't tell me you haven't noticed."

Sharon stopped pushing and swung Linda around so they could talk face to face.

Linda leaned back and tried to focus on her friend.

Sharon went to say something, then began to think about what it felt like when Michael was nearby.

"You may be a hell of a pilot, but you're a little thick when it comes to men." Linda tried to put her hands on the wheels, but the brakes were on. "Where's a mechanic when you need one?"

# CHAPTER 13

*"Oi, Canada!"*

Sharon turned around. She sat at the canteen at Duxford airfield, north of London. The airfield had been built on this flat stretch of farmland during World War I. Sharon's most recent delivery, a brand-new Hurricane, was being fitted for combat inside a hangar where mechanics swarmed over it.

A pilot was raising his coffee cup to her. She recognized him as one of the pilots she'd met at Biggin Hill. His accent was Scottish, his hair the colour of ginger, and he was a foot shorter than Sharon.

She raised her own coffee in greeting. "How are you, Ginger?"

He walked over to sit down across from her. "What're you doin' here, lassie?"

"I could ask the same of you." Sharon watched him warily.

He leaned forward and offered his hand. "My real name is Jock."

"Sharon." She shook his hand. *He has remarkably gentle hands.*

"I was on patrol this mornin'. The engine started actin' up. Puffin' a wee bit of oily smoke. So here we are."

Sharon wrapped her hands around the coffee cup. "For me, it was a Hurricane delivery. Now I'm just waiting for a ride to the next one on my list."

"How many deliveries are they havin' you do in a day?" Jock asked.

"Depends. So far, I've had as many as six and as few as two." Sharon saw Jock's attention shift, and her eyes followed to a nearby barrage balloon. A couple climbed between the rear fins and up the spine of the grey three-finned balloon. Somewhere near the middle, the couple sat down, and the balloon began to rise. "What's going on there?" Sharon turned to Jock.

His face turned red. "Sightseein', I believe."

"Have I embarrassed you?"

Jock shook his head. "What's your tally now? Last time I heard, you had three."

"Word travels fast around the airfields." *I don't like where this is going.* "What's your tally?"

"Four and a half. Why are you changing the subject? Just because you're a bit of a legend among pilots does na mean your exploits are common knowledge to the general population."

Sharon watched the balloon rise. *I wonder where Michael is.* She caught a glimpse of white undergarments. "That couple is sightseeing, you say?"

Jock said, "Once around the block."

"What?"

"A not very polite turn of phrase."

"You mean he's after a bit of crumpet?"

"More or less. I mean, I'm not offerin', just explainin', understand. Wife would have my balls for bookends, you see, if I were to catch a ride on that balloon." Jock's face turned a shade redder.

"Rather an interesting way to mate."

Jock's face was glowing now.

Sharon decided to change the subject. "How come everyone's so interested in my tally?"

Jock thought for a moment. "Suppose it's because you're a bit of a natural. Pilots watch how other pilots fly. When they see you land, it's like you're performin' a bit of magic. Not everyone has the touch, understand. Me, I'm a good shot and a fair pilot. You're a rare one. The aircraft is more like a bird than a machine when you're flyin' it."

It was Sharon's turn to feel the heat of embarrassment on her face.

"But are you a good shot?" Jock asked.

"Shot a few gophers back home. And some clay pigeons."

"Gophers?"

"Ground squirrels. Any advice for someone who's never fired the guns in a fighter plane?"

"Depends what you're askin'."

"You're a good shot. What does it take to shoot down a Nazi?"

Jock looked past her. "Get in close."

"How close?"

Jock looked directly at her. "Very close. Use short bursts. Remember, your bullets drop over distance, so just get within a hundred yards and blast away at the bastards. If you can, hit the cockpit. Then get out before someone gets you."

"Thanks."

"Don't know why you want to know. Fightin's nothing to do with you. You're a woman."

"If the rumours of invasion are true, no one in the Luftwaffe will be taking the time to check. Besides," she winked, "I hear people like us — Canadians and Scots, that is — are cannon fodder for the Empire."

"The rumours are true. I blundered over France, Boulogne, to be exact, a fortnight ago. The flak was murderous, and yes, the port was filled with barges." Jock's eyes lost their focus as he relived the experience. "As far as being cannon fodder up there," he pointed up with his index finger, "no one's takin' the time to check where you're from."

"What were you doing over Boulogne?"

"Chasing a Jerry flyin' a Messerschmitt 109."

"Did you get him?"

"You bet I did. That Nazi bastard killed a friend of mine."

# CHAPTER 14
## [ FRIDAY, AUGUST 16, 1940 ]

**Cannon shells pierced the fuel tank** just ahead of the Spitfire's cockpit.

The fuel tank exploded into flame.

The outside of the cockpit was surrounded with fire. Then the flames entered the cockpit itself. Sharon reached for the harness. Her gloves were on fire as her fingers tried to release the Sutton harness in front of her chest. The thumb and forefinger of her right hand finally pulled the leather thong. The harness fell away from her, freeing her from the seat.

She reached for the canopy release. The canopy slid back. The fire roared when its tongues tasted fresh oxygen.

Sharon rolled the aircraft onto its back and fell away from the crippled fighter. She looked down at her blackened hands and feet. The force of the wind was extinguishing some of the flames on her flight suit. Her stump fingers found the parachute release and she pulled. Agony filled her mind as countless nerve endings sent their screaming messages to her brain.

After the shock of the parachute opening, she swung under the canopy and could smell burnt meat.

An alarm rang.

She looked down at green fields. Her Spitfire trailed smoke and fire. It hit the ground and exploded.

The alarm rang again.

Sharon looked at her hands. They were clenching the bedspread.

She sat up. Her alarm rang. She reached over to turn it off. *I still have fingers.*

In the fresh quiet, she saw particles of dust illuminated by a shaft of sunlight cutting the room in half.

Sweat dripped into her eyes, and she wiped her face with the white sheet. As she closed her eyes, the image of her exploding Spitfire was etched on the inside of her eyelids. She swung her feet out of the bed to feel the coolness of the wooden floor.

Less than an hour later, Mother handed her a chit and a box wrapped with brown paper.

He watched her closely. "It's a football. Never been used. It's my nephew's. He's in North Africa. Every boy wants a football." He held his hands out. "My nephew will be happy to know there's a lad who will be able to give the ball a good workout."

Sharon smiled and handed the package back.

Mother set it down next to him. "I'll have it waiting for you when you get back."

"Mother, you're a sweetheart." She hugged him close and kissed his cheek. He smelled of pipe smoke and aftershave.

"Get on with you. The air taxi is waiting." He waved her away.

"That's a nice blush. What brand of rouge do you use?" She put her hand to his cheek.

"Go!" He smiled and waved her away.

Early in the afternoon, she delivered a Hurricane to Tangmere. It was an airfield on the south coast of England, east of Portsmouth and Chichester. From ten miles away, she could see oily smoke rising above her destination. Her eyes scanned the sky, looking for other aircraft. There were none.

After she dropped down to three hundred feet on finals, she could smell the smoke and cordite. She landed and dodged a bomb crater, then taxied to a hangar that wasn't burning or damaged.

She shut down, switched off, and climbed out of the Hurricane.

"Little warm for that leather jacket and gloves, I expect," some-one said.

*Gives me some protection if there's a fire.* She stepped off the wing and looked around.

An aircraftsman wearing a leather vest and rolled-up sleeves stood at the wing. He was wearing a tie, a shirt, and mud-spattered trousers that were spattered with mud. "We just had a spot of trouble with Jerry. Goering sent over a flock of bloody Stuka dive bombers that did some damage."

Sharon unzipped her leather jacket and pulled off her helmet. She unwrapped the white silk scarf from around her neck and left the ends dangling. "Anybody hurt?"

"At least a dozen killed. Some were civilians." He looked at the burning hangars and the fire crews spraying water on blackened timber and collapsed roofs. "Fighting that fire's a bloody waste of time. There's nothing in there to save. Give us a hand to push the Hurricane into the hangar. Though I'm beginning to wonder if it's safer outside than in."

"Just the two of us?"

He looked over his shoulder. "Do you see anyone else?"

"Where did everyone else go?" Sharon dropped her parachute and jacket on the grass.

"My mates went over to that hangar just before the raid started." He pointed at the wreck, where firemen were pouring water on the ashes.

She closed her eyes and reached for a wing root.

The aircraftsman took the tail. "You know how we're always being told to keep at it? Stiff upper lip. Get on with the job because Hitler is knocking on the door. Well, I suppose that's what I'll have to do."

# CHAPTER 15
## [ SATURDAY, AUGUST 17, 1940 ]

**Sharon hung up her flight suit** and dropped off her parachute in the equipment shed at White Waltham. The inside smelled of dust, mould, and the captive heat of a summer sun.

She shut off the lights and closed the door behind her. Outside, the moonless night wrapped itself around her like a wartime black-out curtain. She looked up. *Now this looks like home.* The stars were almost as bright as she remembered on the prairies.

After about five minutes, her eyes had adjusted to the dark, and she began her walk to the cottage.

Once she had the feel of the tarmac under her feet, she began to relax. Familiar landmarks passed as shadows to her right and left.

The breeze carried the scent of tobacco.

*German paratrooper.* She smiled at her fear. *We're all so paranoid about an invasion.*

She heard the crunch of a heavy boot on the tarmac. The musty stink of cigarettes mixed with body odour.

She stopped. There was movement just ahead of her.

Something sharp and metallic jabbed her between the breasts.

"Step forward." The voice was thickly accented. It wheezed and whistled when it inhaled.

"How the hell can I do that with a bayonet jammed in my chest?"

The pressure at her chest eased, but she could sense steel there, hovering inches away. She had a flashback of Uncle Marmaduke pushing up against her in the storage room. It ignited her.

"Who are you?" the man asked.

"Who the hell are you? I've done six deliveries for the ATA today, and I'm knackered." She shook her head. *Who is this idiot who thinks he can jab me with a bayonet?*

"I'm LDV!" The voice was pitched higher this time.

Sharon heard indignation and ignored it. "If you really are in the Home Guard, shouldn't you be looking for Germans instead of me?"

Silence for a moment. "If you really are ATA, why are you a woman? I've never heard of a woman being a pilot."

"Now you have!"

"How do I know you're not fifth column?" the home guard asked.

"Because I'm a bloody Canadian, you fucking halfwit! Now, get the hell out of my way, and let me get home to get some sleep. I've got a full day ahead of me tomorrow." *Now you've done it — he's going to run you through.*

Silence, then, "Pass. Only a Canadian would be that foul-mouthed."

"Asshole." Sharon stepped to her left and walked forward. The hair stood up along the back of her neck. All the way home, she expected to hear a rifle shot.

# CHAPTER 16
## [ SUNDAY, AUGUST 18, 1940 ]

**She looked for the man from the Home Guard** the next morning when she walked back to White Waltham, but he had disappeared. The feeling of having to watch her back, however, remained.

"There you are!" Mother waved a chit above his head. "Biggin Hill is waiting for you. You'll arrive at the birthday party in style. I mean, who else will be flying to the party in a brand-new Spitfire?"

"You're a magician." Sharon took the piece of paper.

"Don't forget this." Mother handed her the package wrapped in brown paper.

"The soccer ball! Thank you! I'm sure Sean will love it." Sharon tucked the package under her arm.

"I had an unusual conversation with a member of the Home Guard this morning. A Major Pike, retired. Claims he had a run in with a foul-mouthed Canadian girl last night. He seemed to think there weren't any women in the ATA. That it might have been a spy. I put him straight that, yes, we do have some very fine women pilots." Mother hesitated.

"Major Pike, was it? Very good name for him. Poked me in the chest with his bayonet." Sharon pointed to the spot between her breasts.

"So that's what set you off. He didn't tell me that."

Sharon crossed her arms.

Mother leaned on the counter. "He struck me as a popinjay. A real Colonel Blimp. Put a uniform on him, and he struts around like a member of the palace guard. Still, try not to offend the old sod. He does have a rifle, and, judging by the thickness of his glasses, poor eyesight."

Sharon frowned. *What the hell is a popinjay?*

"A windbag," Mother said.

"You and Linda have a very annoying habit of reading my mind." Sharon hefted her gear and Sean's present.

"It's your face. Whatever you're thinking is written on it. Try looking inscrutable." Mother struck a pose.

Sharon chuckled as she walked toward the duty Anson. She turned her face to the sun. *I'm really looking forward to this.*

It was cloudy and near midday when she saw Biggin Hill from about fifteen miles out. This time, she'd kept her altitude at one thousand feet and her eyes alert for other aircraft.

Three minutes later, the Spitfire's wheels kissed the runway. She worked the rudder to guide the aircraft in the direction of her father's hangar. When the tail dropped and she was at taxi speed, Sharon wove back and forth so that she could see around the fighter's Merlin engine.

She shut down and switched off on the concrete to one side of a Belfast hangar. Its massive wooden doors were open, and a Spitfire was being wheeled out under the arched roof.

An aircraftsman climbed onto the wing and grabbed the edge of Sharon's open cockpit. "Switches off?"

"Yes." Sharon released her Sutton harness and opened the side door.

Three aircraftsmen appeared and guided her Spitfire into the hangar.

The tires squealed on the polished concrete floor. They swung its nose around so it faced out. On each wing, the panels were opened to access the machine gun compartments.

Sharon climbed out and retrieved Sean's gift.

"Hello there. Sean will be happy to finally meet you."

Sharon turned around to stand face to face with Patrick O'Malley. "Hello, Dad."

O'Malley smiled. "The party is in two hours. I have a few things to do before we trot up to Leaves Green. It looks to be another busy day."

"Leaves Green?" Sharon held the soccer ball out in front of her.

"We live just up the road." O'Malley pointed northwest. "A ten-minute walk."

Sharon handed O'Malley the ball. "I hope he likes to play football. We call it soccer back home."

"The boy is mad about his sports. Doesn't stop runnin' from the time he gets up in the mornin' 'til it gets dark."

A man stuck his head out of the back office door. "Scramble!"

O'Malley and Sharon automatically looked east and scanned the sky.

The air-raid siren wailed.

A pilot was running for the Spitfire parked on the concrete apron.

O'Malley ran to the aircraft. He stopped, turned, and pointed. "There's a slit trench around the side. Get in it!"

The pilot stepped onto the wing, lifted himself up, and settled into the cockpit.

O'Malley was there to help strap the pilot in.

The pilot asked, "The machine guns are synchronized to one hundred yards?"

"Just as you requested," O'Malley said.

Sharon watched as Spitfires and Hurricanes began to start up and take off in ones and twos.

"Clear!" the pilot said.

O'Malley stepped off the wing and ran down alongside the fuselage.

The propeller turned.

*He's flooded the engine,* Sharon thought as the stink of raw fuel filled the air.

The propeller stopped.

The hum of approaching aircraft made Sharon look east. Anti-aircraft guns began to open up.

Sharon looked to her right. A woman who might have weighed a hundred pounds was sitting on a metal seat at the rear of one of the guns. She wore fatigues and a helmet. She pressed a pedal. The gun erupted.

"Go!" O'Malley took her by the elbow.

She ran to the corner of the hangar with her parachute banging at the backs of her legs and stopped to turn and see if he was behind her when she reached the corner. *Christ, I didn't take my parachute off.*

O'Malley was on the fighter's wing again. He was helping the pilot out of his Spitfire.

Her father and the pilot jumped down off the wing.

A string of bombs exploded with one deafening *crump* after another. Clods of earth and clouds of dust were thrown into the air.

A Dornier 17, with its glass nose and green-grey camouflage, was fifty feet off the ground and headed their way. She could see the gunner as he opened up. White-tailed tracer bullets reached out to them.

Some bullets whizzed overtop of the Spitfire. Others whined past her as they skipped off the concrete. One ricocheted past her nose.

Sharon dropped down to one knee and watched Patrick as he turned to run toward her.

She saw a startled look come over her father's face.

O'Malley fell onto his knees and coughed up blood. He leaned forward. His head touched the ground. There were two holes in the back of his coveralls.

"Run, you daft bitch!" The pilot ran past Sharon.

O'Malley rolled onto his side.

*This isn't happening.* Sharon jumped up and ran to her father.

The Dornier screamed overhead with its guns still firing. The ground heaved as a bomb exploded on the other side of the hangar. Sharon was knocked to the ground. She crawled forward on her hands and knees.

Another Dornier flew over the runway and dropped its bombs.

Sharon crawled next to her father and looked down. She smelled copper and iron. Her father's blood was pooling on the concrete. Blood covered his chest and chin. His eyes stared past her.

She bent over to touch his forehead. He did not react.

His eyes remained open.

Sharon dropped the soccer ball and looked at the Spitfire. She looked down at O'Malley. He stared at infinity.

The anti-aircraft gun fired. Sharon felt the concussion against her ribs and looked to her right. The woman sitting at the trigger was pointing and screaming. Sharon looked up. One of the bombers was trailing smoke and fire. It lost altitude as it flew north and west.

Sharon raced to the Spitfire, climbed onto the wing, and eased herself into the cockpit.

She put on her Sutton harness.

Going through her preflight checks, she primed the engine.

"Clear!" The voice sounded like it came from someone else.

One of the aircraftsmen operated the starter balanced on an oversized pair of wheels.

Another bomb exploded.

She switched on. The shockwave from the bomb made the Spitfire rock from side to side. The propeller turned. The engine coughed black smoke. It hesitated, then caught, and she eased the throttle forward.

The aircraftsman disengaged the starter and rolled it away. He waved at her before running for cover.

Sharon applied rudder.

To her left, she saw a straight line without any bomb craters and enough room for her takeoff. She swung the nose around and lined up.

"Throttle!"

The Spitfire accelerated. She looked up.

The first wave of low-level bombers was gone.

She aimed for a stand of trees at the far side of the field. She pushed the stick forward. The tail lifted. She looked along either side of the nose, trying to spot any bomb craters.

The wheels skipped along the grass. She eased back on the stick, applied the brakes, and retracted the undercarriage.

Grief reached up with its hot hands and threatened to overwhelm her. It was difficult to breathe. She reached for the oxygen mask and put it on.

Sharon went through her checks: pitch, mixture, undercarriage, engine temperature, oxygen, gun sight. . . *For Christ's sake, turn on the gun sight. Shit! Where is it?* She found the switch and turned it on.

Sharon caught a glint of sunlight on the Perspex. To her right, a pair of twin-engined Dornier bombers were rising and falling over the contours of the ground as they ran away from Biggin Hill and back to France.

"Get in close, short bursts, watch your tail." She said it over and over again.

"Watch out for the Hun in the sun!" She held up two fingers in the middle of the sun's glare and checked for predators.

She climbed to get above the Dorniers. To hide in the sun.

Two thousand feet above them, she looked up and checked the mirror, then the sky on either side. "Go!" She dove in a long split S turn to get on the tail of the trailing bomber.

She glanced to see her thumb on the trigger. *Get close and use short bursts, just like Jock told you.*

The controls were getting heavier as her speed increased.

The wings of the trailing Dornier filled the rings of the gun sight. She waited, then fired a short burst. She felt the recoil of eight machine guns. The Spitfire slowed.

The tracer bullets fell in a gentle arc below the bomber's tail.

She raised the nose and was dragged down into the seat as the G forces increased.

Another short burst.

The tracer bullets ripped into the fuselage and worked their way up into the cockpit. The bomber turned right. Bits of debris floated behind the Nazi.

Sharon pulled away, turned, and gained altitude. She looked down.

The first Dornier nosed into the ground. A mushroom of flame and black smoke rose into the sky. Sharon looked for the leading bomber.

*There!* It was turning beneath her, trying to hide in the blind spot under her belly.

She reversed her turn, rolled onto her back, and dove to get on the Dornier's tail.

This time, tracer bullets reached out to her as the gunner behind the cockpit fired in defense. She wove right and left as she gained on the Dornier.

This time, she got in closer and attacked from one side.

Sharon aimed for where the fuselage met the graceful wings. She could see the yellow paint on the engine cowlings and the black crosses on the wingtips.

Her thumb pressed the trigger.

This time, she was expecting the recoil from the machine guns as the Spitfire slowed. The tracer bullets dove into the fuselage and into the glass cockpit. The enemy gunner stopped firing.

She touched the rudder. The bullets walked across the wing and hit the bomber's engine. Black smoke and flame erupted.

"Too close!" Sharon leaned hard right on the stick, pulled out, and climbed. She held her breath until the g-forces eased.

She looked below. The second Dornier turned on its back, hit a stand of trees, and exploded.

Sharon checked the sky, turned, and climbed.

Above, a second wave of bombers approached Biggin Hill. She checked the sun for any fighters hiding above her.

The Spitfire climbed steadily until it was between the sun and the higher-level formation of twin-engined German bombers. She recognized the silhouettes of Junkers 88s. She weaved in and out, continually checking above and behind her Spitfire for enemy fighters.

She looked down at the formation. *The Junkers 88 has guns in its belly, but not in its tail.*

Sharon eased the stick forward and turned left to get into position behind the formation. She glanced in the rearview mirror. "Clear."

She used the speed of the dive to catch up with the last bomber. *These Junkers are fast. Remember, short bursts. There can't be much ammunition left.*

Sharon gained on the trailing bomber. She saw its black crosses and radial engines. She lightly tapped the rudder and pressed the button.

Her tracer bullets hit the bomber between the right engine and the cockpit. Debris flew back at her. She pulled right, then left.

As she passed the bomber, she saw flame licking back along the wing from a ruptured fuel tank. The bomber dropped out of formation. A body fell away, then another. One parachute blossomed.

She attacked the next bomber from the opposite side. Her first brief burst fell well behind the bomber. The Junkers turned away from her.

She followed — aiming for the spot in the sky where the Junkers was headed — and fired.

It flew into the tracer. A shudder went through the aircraft.

Sharon fired another burst. The bomber filled her windscreen.

As she flew over the bomber's right wing, Sharon glanced left and saw blood spattered inside the shattered cockpit. The crippled Junkers dove for the earth.

She pulled back on the stick. The weight of the g-forces induced a wave of nausea.

A flashback of her father coughing blood and his empty, staring eyes made her shudder with the realization that the same thing had just happened to the men in the bomber.

She gained altitude. "One more attack." Sharon looked up into the sun.

A pair of wing tips appeared at the edges of the sun's blinding core.

*Here it comes!* Her mind filled with a profound sense of clarity. *Don't dive. He'll have you then.* She turned and climbed to face the fighter diving down out of the sun.

In this head-on rush, the closing speed was over five hundred miles an hour.

She hunched down, pulled her shoulders in tight. Tracer bullets passed over the top of her canopy.

Sharon fired. The Spitfire slowed with the recoil. Her guns stopped firing. "Shit! I'm out of ammunition!"

The pale belly of the Messerschmitt flashed overhead. Its engine coughed smoke.

Sharon rolled her Spitfire onto its back. Dust and a clot of mud from the floor fell upward against the canopy. Her eyes watched the dirt as it bounced against the Perspex, then fell into her lap when she righted her aircraft to follow the Messerschmitt 109. It was half a mile ahead and trailing a white line of coolant and smoke.

Sharon gradually closed the distance. *If I get on his tail, he won't be able to shoot at me. He can't know that I'm out of ammunition.*

The Messerschmitt 109 turned east.

Sharon turned with him. He continued the turn and headed inland.

Sharon found herself within a quarter mile and closing rapidly. *His engine must be packing it in.*

She throttled back and closed to within one hundred yards. His cockpit was at the centre of her ring site. She saw him looking back over his shoulder.

Sharon closed to seventy-five yards. Spatters of oil from the 109's engine appeared on her windscreen.

The 109 turned right. She followed and closed. There was a whiff of the German's exhaust mixed in with the stink of burning rubber and oil.

Something flew back from the Messerschmitt. Sharon watched his canopy float up and over her Spitfire.

A large piece of debris fell away from the enemy aircraft.

*Wham!*

The Spitfire began shuddering. The control stick hit her hard on the inside of her right knee. She grabbed it with both hands.

She looked ahead.

The 109 was gone.

She throttled back. The vibration eased.

Sharon looked for a place to land and saw Biggin Hill to the west. Columns of smoke rose up from the airfield.

*Ease the throttle back some more. Go through your pre-landing checks.*

She tapped the throttle back and set the flaps at one quarter. "There," she said as the vibration became even less pronounced.

"Wheels down." As her airspeed dropped further, Sharon felt the aircraft returning to her control.

"Throttle all the way back." The vibration almost disappeared.

When she knew she was going to make the runway, she slid back the canopy. "Pick a line that won't put you into a bomb crater." Sharon pulled back on the stick and held the fighter off until it stalled at four or five inches off of the runway. The wheels kissed the ground. She rolled up to within fifty feet of her father's hangar and shut down.

She released her harness and opened the door. Sharon looked to her left. Patrick's body lay under a blanket on the concrete apron in front of the hangar. She climbed out onto the wing.

"What the hell have you been up to?"

Sharon looked in the direction of the voice. She spotted William. He had his hands on his hips. His face was streaked with dirt and tears.

Sharon shrugged and looked away from her father's body.

William pushed back his brown hair. "What happened to your propeller, and who fired those guns?"

Sharon looked at the propeller. One blade was bent back by ten or fifteen degrees, and the spinner was gone. *That explains the vibration.*

"Well?" William asked. "Who fired the guns?"

Sharon looked at him. "I did."

"Did you get one of the bastards?"

Sharon found herself looking at her hands. "Actually, more than one."

William wasn't looking at her. He pointed at the nose of her Spitfire. He walked closer.

Sharon stepped to the ground and walked around the wing. She could hear the engine ticking as it cooled.

William pulled a rag from his pocket and wiped it along the underside of the engine cowling.

"What is it?"

"What did you hit?" William asked.

"Two Dorniers and two Junkers. There was a 109 as well, but I didn't see what happened to him. I got in behind him, but by then I was out of ammunition. A chunk of debris fell off of him, and I flew right into it." Sharon caught the scent of something wafting around the aircraft. It smelled familiar. Her mouth filled with saliva.

William turned to look at her. "You shot down four?"

Sharon shrugged. "Yes. I did."

"But what did you hit?" William opened the rag. It was stained with blood.

Sharon sagged. *Oh my God.* She looked under her Spitfire. Red drops were falling on the concrete.

"How close were you to his tail?"

*His canopy came off, then something hit the propeller of my aircraft.*

"It looks like a Jerry pilot went through your propeller." He bent down to look under her wing. "There's a piece of him stuck in the radiator."

Sharon shook her head. The grief of her father's death, the horror of what she'd done, all of it seemed to hit her like a blow to the chest. She found it difficult to breathe.

"Come over here." William sat her down at the side of the hangar in one of two chairs leaning up against the grey brick wall. "Back in a tick."

Sharon watched as a Bedford truck pulled up. Two men put her father's body on a stretcher and slid it into the back of the truck. She could see at least two other stretchers there.

"Have a taste of this. Patrick kept it in his desk drawer." William handed her a glass. He poured from the bottle.

"What is it?"

"Rum. The good stuff." William stopped pouring and waited for her to drink.

"Aren't you going to have some?" Sharon raised her glass.

"To Patrick." William lifted the bottle to his lips and drank.

Sharon tipped the glass back. She could feel the rum run its hot course down into her stomach. *The warmth feels better*, she thought as her eyes watered.

"Christ, that was close. I didn't notice 'til just now." William used the bottle to point at Sharon's Spitfire.

Sharon looked at the fuselage behind the cockpit. A neat row of holes were punched in and around the roundel, starting just behind the wing root and working their way up to the tail.

William looked at her. "You weren't joking, were you? You shot down four bombers and a 109."

Sharon shrugged. "Yes. It happened."

William shook his head and took another swig from the bottle.

"You there!"

William and Sharon turned.

An officer stood with his hands on his hips and braid up his sleeves. "We haven't got bloody time for a drink! The bastards are sure to be back. We've got to be prepared! Where the hell is O'Malley?"

Sharon pointed in the general direction of the departed truck. "They just took him away."

"Where the hell did he go? We have Spitfires and Hurricanes to refuel and rearm!"

William said, "He was killed, sir. Jerry machine-gunned him. You're standing in his blood. We were givin' Patrick a toast."

The officer looked down, frowned, and stepped to his left. "And who is this?" He pointed at Sharon.

William said, "A pilot. In fact, an ace. And she's O'Malley's daughter."

"What kind of rot is that?" the officer said.

Sharon stood up with her feet shoulder-width apart.

William pointed at her Spitfire. "She just landed. Shot down four bombers and, if I'm not mistaken, that's blood on the belly of the Spit. The fifth one was a 109 pilot who bailed out and hit her propeller."

"You mean to tell me that girl just shot down five of the bastards?" The officer shook his head in disbelief.

Sharon looked to her right and saw the brown paper wrapping on the soccer ball. She walked over and picked it up.

"Where are you going?" the officer asked.

She looked at William. "To a birthday party in Leaves Green."

"Haven't you heard? One of the Jerry bombers crashed into the village. Who knows what you'll find. It's a bloody shambles there, too." The officer pointed to the north to emphasize his point.

o **"Right over there."** The fire warden wore a helmet, a faded, khaki-coloured World War I army uniform, and a grey moustache. He pointed to half of a row of four houses. The furthest half of the two-storey, side-by-side homes stood straight and white in the sun. The nearest half was rubble. The twin-finned aft section of a Dornier bomber lay to one side in the back garden. Its swastikas were still visible on the fins.

"Which home was Patrick O'Malley's?" Sharon asked.

The fire warden lifted his helmet. "The one on this end what got hit by the bastards." He walked away.

Sharon looked at the pile of wood, brick, and shattered glass. The

front door of the nearest home hung open like a drunken guest leaning on the doorstep.

A woman stepped out of the bakery with a bag. She was wearing a
flowered dress and her grey hair was tied back. She saw Sharon and
walked over. "How are you, love?"

Sharon looked at the soccer ball tucked under her arm. "Late for a
birthday party." She tried to smile.

"That was the only lucky thing about what happened. The plane
crashed about an hour before Sean's party was to start. All the children
'round here were invited." The woman shifted her bag to the other arm.

"Has anyone seen Sean?"

"His mother, Hazel, was just outside the front door when the bomber
crashed. She was thrown out into the street. They took her body away.
Sean was inside. I don't know how Patrick will take the news."

"He's dead."

The woman put her free hand to her chest just below her throat.
"The whole family is gone, then?"

Sharon looked at the woman. "What's your name?"

"Margaret."

"Was Sean's body found?"

"What's your name, then?"

"Sharon." She looked down at her flight suit and realized for the
first time how out of place she must appear.

"Patrick's Sharon?"

"That's right."

"Sean was so looking forward to meeting you. He talked of nothing else this past week."

Sharon handed the soccer ball to Margaret. "Will you hang onto
this for me?"

Margaret took the ball. "What are you going to do?"

"I think my father would like to be buried with his son and his
wife." Sharon walked closer to the rubble. She turned to Margaret.
"Where was the kitchen?"

Margaret moved closer, put the packages down on the sidewalk,
and walked past Sharon. "This way."

Sharon followed.

"Why the kitchen?"

"If there was a cake, and Hazel went outside, well, he probably went for a taste of the icing. I know that's what I would have done."

Margaret lifted her skirt to her knees and stepped over a pile of debris. "Right about there, I should think." She pointed.

"Thank you." Sharon unzipped the top of her flight suit, pulled her arms out, and tied the flight suit arms around her waist. Then she loosened her tie and pulled it off. Sticking it in a pocket, she said, "No time like the present."

Sharon bent and took a brick in each hand, tossing them into what had once been a back garden. One of the bricks bounced and banged up against the Dornier's fuselage. It made a satisfying thunk.

"Fucking Nazis!" She picked up a brick, aimed at the swastika on the tail, and fired. The brick flew overtop of the tail. "Goddamned cancer!" She picked up another brick and threw it. It missed to the right and swished though a bush. "Shitty war!" Sharon picked up a third brick.

"Does it help?"

Sharon turned.

"Nigel Brown." He held out his right hand. His left was tucked in the pocket of his grey work pants. His tan work shirt was rolled up at the sleeves. He was over six feet tall. He had a five o'clock shadow and a round face.

Sharon stepped down off the pile and felt the calluses on his hand as she shook it. "Sharon Lacey."

Nigel looked at the wreckage and kicked at a brick with his work-boot. He rubbed a hand over his bristles. "You were saying?"

Sharon shrugged. "Nothing useful."

"You're a pilot, I see," Nigel said.

"Yes." *What does he want?*

"Patrick told me you were coming today. Your father and I were neighbours." Nigel surveyed the wreckage.

"Where's your house?" Sharon looked over to the houses still standing.

"Next-door neighbours."

"Oh." Sharon looked at the rubble. "Did you live alone?"

"Margaret's my wife. She wasn't home at the time. I was at work." Nigel shook his head. "Fucking war."

"Yes." Sharon turned, bent at the waist, and picked up a piece of wood. She tossed it into the backyard. It made a clunk as it hit the swastika on the tail of the Dornier. "Fuckers!"

Nigel moved to her right and grunted as he picked up a section of roof. "Give us a hand."

Sharon grabbed the opposite corner, and they dragged the weight into the backyard.

"Margaret says you think Sean was in the kitchen." Nigel wiped his hands across the front of his pants.

Sharon nodded. "It was his birthday. When I was eleven, if my mother went outside, I'd be in the kitchen getting a taste of cake." She closed her eyes with a memory of her mother handing her a bowl with the remains of the icing. She licked her lips and smiled.

Nigel chuckled. "If memory serves, that would be my objective as well."

Sharon felt sweat trickling down her back as she bent to pick up more debris. "Why are you here?"

"Margaret and I have no children of our own. Sean and I were friends. When he wanted to chat, he would often come over to our home."

Sharon hefted a clump of four bricks still held together with mortar. She heaved the load, then looked over her shoulder to see it whiz past Nigel. "Sorry."

"Why are you here?" Nigel asked.

"Sean's birthday!" She bent back to grab another brick. *Don't be angry with him. He's trying to help.*

"No, why are you in England? You sound American."

"Canadian. My mother died. I came to meet my father and my mother's family. So far, it hasn't worked out very well." Sharon threw more bricks on the pile in the backyard. *At this rate, we might find Sean in a week.* She stretched her back and looked at the sky, where vapour trails etched the course of another air battle. Every so often, she could hear the chatter of machine guns.

An hour later, she stood and closed her eyes as a swell of dizziness washed over her.

"Margaret has organized some tea for us." Nigel put his hand on her shoulder.

Sharon nodded and went to sit on the curb next to the front step — all that remained of her father's house. She saw a puddle of dried blood in the middle of the road. *Must be Hazel's.* This was followed by a flashback of blood pooling under the nose of her Spitfire. And next to that, on the concrete, her father's blood.

She looked up and saw that a dozen people now worked on the rubble. "I didn't realize so many people came to help."

"What's that?" Margaret carried a basket and was followed by two other women. "My sisters, Maxine and Geraldine."

Sharon nodded at the pair of women, who smiled at her. They both wore dresses. "Thank you."

"Where's Paddy O'Malley? Down at the pub while all of you do the digging?" The voice came from behind the sisters.

Sharon turned in the direction of the voice.

A man and a woman stood arm in arm. He wore a new green army uniform and she a blue dress. "Is he stuck in a bog somewhere?"

Sharon stood.

Margaret set down her basket and stood next to Sharon. "He's dead. Killed during today's raid on Biggin Hill."

The woman in the blue dress pulled at the soldier's arm, but he stood his ground. "Won't get any sympathy from me. Bloody RAF left us at the mercy of the Luftwaffe at Dunkirk!"

Maxine took Sharon's hand. "Every town has one. Goes to the pub in the afternoon and in the evening comes out looking for a fight. Sit down and have summat to eat."

"Time for tea." Geraldine lifted a red-checked tablecloth out of the basket.

Maxine and Margaret spread the cloth on the sidewalk and set out plates of sandwiches.

The soldier said, "Leave the Irish bastard to rot!"

Rage blossomed in Sharon. *Leave it alone.*

"The bastards were cannon fodder in the last war. Let the Irish do the same in this one!" The soldier made a fist and shook it at the women.

Sharon shook off Maxine's grip and covered half the distance to the soldier before anyone had time to react.

The soldier's girlfriend turned when she heard Sharon's approach. "Peter!"

The soldier turned. He stumbled back when he spotted Sharon.

"Asshole!" Sharon cocked her right arm and kicked with her left leg.

Her fist caught Peter on the nose. Her left foot caught him square in the belly. Peter hit the ground. She found herself sitting on his chest, her fists mechanically driving blows into Peter's face. "You son of a bitch!" She smelled the alcohol on him. It was fuel for her rage.

Someone grabbed her around the neck and shoulders and pulled her back. She kicked at the soldier and missed.

Nigel said, "That wanker's hardly worth it. But it was fun to watch. You're a tiger, Sharon. Patrick would be proud of you." He dragged her back. "We don't have time or energy for this. Look at your hands. How are you going to get Sean out if you waste all of your anger and strength on the likes of Peter here?"

Sharon looked down at her fists. The knuckles were smeared with blood. She hung her head.

"Bitch broke my nose!" Peter stood up, supported by his girlfriend. "I'm gettin' the constable!" He pulled away from his girlfriend's hand and marched down the road. His ankle turned and he fell sideways into the gutter.

Margaret took Sharon by the elbow. "Come on, let's get you cleaned up." They walked over to the bakery. The owner greeted them at the door.

"We need to get this one cleaned up," Margaret said.

"Sink's at the back." The baker pointed with a white finger. "Makin' a fresh batch of bread for you."

"Thanks," Sharon said.

They found the sink. Margaret turned on the taps. Sharon winced as the water hit her raw knuckles. "Ooh. Everyone is being so nice, and I get into a fight."

"Actually, there's not much you can do wrong in this village."

"What?" Sharon looked at Margaret.

"Word from Biggin Hill is you shot down five Huns today. Two more people from the village were killed at Biggin Hill today. Add those to Hazel and Sean, and we've got a funeral for sixteen tomorrow at the chapel. People around here are happy to hear that someone is hitting back against the Nazis." Margaret looked for a towel.

"Still, beating up one of the local soldiers is hardly the best way of showing my gratitude." Sharon shook the water off her hands and took the offered towel. "Thanks."

"Peter was a bully as a child, and he's a bully of a man. He survived Dunkirk and can't understand why the town didn't welcome him as a hero. Sits down at the pub and expects everyone there will buy him drinks. Fact is, most of us still can't stomach him." Margaret crossed her arms. "Now, let's get some food into you before you fall over."

Sharon ate two sandwiches and, when she found there was coffee, drank three cups.

Maxine handed her another sandwich. "Try my cucumbers. Grew them in the back garden. A very good crop, if I do say so."

"Thanks." Sharon unwrapped the waxed paper and took a bite. There was a sweet taste of ripe vegetable mixed with salt, encased in fresh bread. "Very good." She swallowed and took another bite.

"When did you eat last?" Maxine tucked her hands between her knees into the folds of her blue dress.

Sharon covered her mouth. "This morning."

"It's nearly eight o'clock," Maxine said.

Sharon looked at the wrecked building and aircraft. "A lot has happened since this morning."

"Sean was such a friendly boy. If I close my eyes, I can see him and his parents walking down the street. They were a happy family. Sean always looked up to his father." The evening sun highlighted Maxine's red hair.

Sharon nodded. "I would have liked to have met him."

Maxine said, "He had hair your colour, and blue eyes. So much energy. That boy was going morning, noon, and night. Made his teachers earn their pay."

Sharon looked at the sun as it touched the tops of the trees. The breeze had moved on and left behind still evening air. "I'd better get back to work. Thank you for the sandwiches."

"Happy to do it."

Four hours later, Sharon stopped and looked around her. She saw only Nigel bending to pull at a broken beam. They worked by the light of three lanterns spaced in a triangle around the rubble. They'd gotten used to working in half-light and deep shadow.

"Why don't you go and get some rest?" Sharon's body ached and the skin on her fingers felt like it had been peeled off.

"I'll quit when you do." He pulled a beam free and dragged it over to the pile in the backyard. Nigel disappeared into the darkness.

She heard the beam thump as it landed on the pile. "I can't stop until I find him."

He walked back into the light of the lanterns. "Let's break for a cup of tea, then we'll get back to it." Nigel stepped over a twisted bed frame.

Sharon walked over to the curb and sat down. *Every muscle and bone aches.* She looked at her hands. She felt the blister bubbles on her palms.

Nigel sat down next to her, then reached for the flask and two cups Margaret had left for them. He handed her a cup and poured.

"Thank you." Sharon took a sip. The tea was too strong and too sweet. Still, it tasted delicious in her parched mouth.

Nigel poured himself a cup and drank. "How's yours?"

"Delicious."

"Mine's bloody awful."

Sharon heard someone tapping on a stone. "Who else is here?"

Nigel turned around. "Ow." He moved his head in a circle to work out the kink in his neck. "Just the two of us."

"Then what's that sound?" She turned to Nigel. "Are you making that sound?"

"Not me."

"Where's it coming from?" Sharon got up. "Quick, before it stops!" Fear clamped its jaws around her heart and squeezed the breath out of her lungs. Her head spun. She had to concentrate to breathe. They walked side by side toward the corner of the partially exposed foundation.

Nigel pointed. "There, I think. You know, you may have been right. That's where they had the kitchen table. It was next to the window. The table was a massive thing. It's possible, if Sean got under it, that he could still be alive."

Sharon pulled a stone away from the side of the pile.

"Careful now." Nigel put a hand on Sharon's shoulder. "We don't want to bring the whole mess down on top of him or us. First, we have to move the lanterns."

Sharon went to get one of them. The lamp hissed as she handed it to Nigel. He took it and found a spot to maximize visibility.

She left and returned with the next two.

"That should do it." Nigel pulled tentatively at a bed frame, then dragged it away. "We work together from now on. Each move must be well thought out." He handed the metal frame to her and she set it in the yard.

Every half hour or so, they switched positions. One would stand at the edge of the pile and hand the debris to the other, who would carry it away.

They worked and waited to see if the tapping would start up again. Tap, tap. Tap, tap, tap.

"There it is again." Sharon held her hand up.

"We have to let him know we're here." Nigel picked up a small shovel and tapped it against a stone jammed low on the pile.

The tapping from inside came back faster, louder.

Sharon cupped her hands around her mouth. "Sean! It's Sharon! We're here. Nigel and I are here!" She felt something building in her. *He's alive! We need to get him out now!*

The tapping stopped for a minute, then picked up again.

Nigel said, "We have to take some tea now."

"What?" Sharon looked at him like he'd lost his mind.

"We're both exhausted. Just a short rest. We're at risk of hurting the boy or worse if we make a mistake now. Our minds have to be as clear as possible."

Sharon looked at the wall of rubble rising above them. One piece taken from the wrong place at the wrong time would bring the entire mess down on top of them. "All right."

They drank and ate quietly, listening in case the tapping started up again. After ten minutes, Nigel nodded to her and they stood.

This time, they worked with fingertips, brushing around bricks, pulling each one out slowly, waiting for a shift in rubble warning them of a cave-in.

The tapping started, slowed, and stopped.

Sharon looked at her fingernails. They were worn down to the quick.

They worked in the mouth of an opening just above the foundation. She and Nigel took turns holding the lantern as they tunneled toward where they hoped to find Sean.

Sharon touched a round, vertical piece of oak. "Can you bring the light a little closer?"

"What have you got?" Nigel eased the lantern in so they could see the exposed table leg. "Looks promising. Work slowly now. We don't know how much room he's got."

Sharon tapped a stone on the table leg.

There was tapping from the other side.

She put her hand on the oak leg. She could feel the tapping being telegraphed onto the blisters on her palm. The pain focused her. "Sean?"

The words from the other side were too muffled to be understood.

Sharon lay on her belly, digging away on either side of the table leg. The dust got into her nostrils and she sneezed. There was the scent of earth and wood. *There's some other smell there, too. Urine! Did I wet myself?*

Dirt and debris fell away under her fingertips.

Sharon sneezed in the cloud of dust particles illuminated by the lantern's glare.

"Bless you." The child's voice was clear.

"Sean?" Sharon asked.

"Who are you?"

"Sharon."

Sean asked, "Where's my father and mother?"

"Sean?" Nigel had his hand on Sharon's boot.

"Nigel?" Sean asked.

"Sharon and I are going to get you out. How much room have you got in there?" Nigel asked.

"I can move my arms and legs," Sean said.

Sharon reached through the opening. "Can you touch my hand?"

At first, she felt a brushing, light as a sparrow's wings, then a child's hands gripped hers. She said, "Okay, let go of me. We're going to move some more of this shit away and make the opening big enough."

"Let me have a go," Nigel said.

"I've got five more minutes in me." Sharon felt the grit in her hair and blinked away the dust on her eyelashes. She reached out with her right hand and pulled at the edges of the opening. She pulled the debris back down along her ribs and hip, then pushed it along her thigh to her knees. Sharon felt Nigel's fingers against her shins and ankles as he pulled the rubble away.

When her fingers brushed the bottom edge of the tabletop, she said, "Nigel, can you hand me the torch?"

She felt the flashlight tap her right knee. Sharon took it and maneuvered it up next to her face. She pressed the button.

A pair of blue eyes and a face the colour of dust stared back at her. His eyes were caked with dirt. She could smell him, too.

"We'll have you out soon," Sharon said.

Sean shook his head. "No."

"What?"

"I'm not coming out." Sean set his jaw in the sharp light of the flashlight.

Sharon took a deep breath. *We don't have time for this.* Then she caught the strong stink of urine. "No one cares that you pee your pants. All we want is to get you safely out of here."

Sean looked back at her. There were tears in his eyes. "My parents. They're dead, aren't they? That's why you wouldn't answer me."

Sharon nodded. "I was with Patrick when he died."

"What happened?"

"A bomber strafed us. He was killed in front of me."

Sean began to sob.

Sharon used the flashlight to guide her hands. She moved debris and dirt around her body and passed it back to Nigel.

She touched Sean's hand.

He looked up.

"Hold onto my wrist. We're going to try to pull you out now." Sharon looked back at Nigel, whose face was at her feet. "Can you pull me out when I tell you to?"

Nigel nodded. "Give the word."

Sharon took Sean by the wrists. "Okay."

Nigel grunted as he pulled.

*Just concentrate on hanging on to Sean.*

She felt her shoulder muscles straining. *Hold on!*

Sean began to slide toward her.

Her right hipbone scraped over the corner of a protruding brick.

Sean pulled through the opening.

*Hold on!*

Dirt choked her. Then a gasp of fresh air. A brick caught her under the chin.

"You're out!" Nigel said.

She released Sean, sat up, and used her sleeve to wipe the dirt and snot from her nose and mouth.

Sean was on his hands and knees.

Nigel held out his hand to the boy. "Come on, Sean. Let's get some food in you and get you cleaned up."

Sharon stood up and looked at the horizon. The sky was turning from black to orange.

"Are you coming?" Sean stood waiting for Sharon. She followed.

# CHAPTER 17
[ MONDAY, AUGUST 19, 1940 ]

**The sweet stink of rotting meat** rose up from the mass grave at the chapel at Biggin Hill.

*That's why there's such a rush to get this over with. Too many dead and nowhere to put them.* Sharon felt Sean lean closer against her hip.

From the other side, Margaret nudged Sharon.

There was a question on Sharon's face when she turned to Margaret.

Margaret mouthed, "Put your arm around the boy."

Sharon looked at Sean, who stared into the row of fifteen coffins arranged side by side at the bottom of the trench. She put her arm around his shoulder and pulled him close. He tucked his head against her ribs. He smelled of soap and the hand-me-down jacket, shirt, and pants Nigel had managed to procure from another family in the village.

Sharon felt him shift and tug up pants that required a belt and another year of growth before they would fit him. *I feel so protective toward him already. It's like I fell in love with him when I saw his dirty face in the midst of all this ruin.*

She looked across the mass grave at the minister. He wore white and black robes and read from his Bible. Above the coffins, people stood with their heads bent, apparently intent on what the minister was saying. Sharon counted the coffins again. "Fifteen."

Sean looked up at her. She shook her head and tried to smile. Sean snuggled closer to her.

*I killed at least that many yesterday.* She remembered the blood on her Spitfire. *The German pilot went through a meat grinder.*

A vivid image of the Me 109 pilot's body exploding into a red mist of flesh, bone, and blood filled her mind's eye. Sharon closed her eyes and suppressed an urge to giggle. *What is wrong with me?*

Sean tugged at her hand. She looked down.

Sean looked away and said, "It's over."

He and Sharon watched the mourners leaving the gravesite. Some looked up into the sky as if expecting another attack.

"Coming with us, Sean?" Margaret asked.

Sean looked at his sister. "He's staying with me." *We never discussed this, never planned beyond the funeral.*

Margaret and Nigel looked at Sharon, then at Sean. "We just thought," Margaret said. "We can offer him a safe home."

*And you think I can't?* Sharon shook her head. "You've been so kind. I . . . we'll never forget. It's just that he's all I've got. I'm all he has. I'm not saying this very well."

Margaret nodded, a frown on her lips.

*He's my brother. I'm his sister. It's that simple.*

Sean looked up at his sister. "Where are you taking me, then?"

*I don't know. We have to go back to White Waltham. He can stay with me there.*

"Somewhere safe." Nigel said. "Sean needs to be somewhere safe. It's not safe around here anymore."

**○ Sharon couldn't help but be impressed.** Spitfires and Hurricanes crackled overhead as they landed or taxied across Biggin Hill's repaired runway. Rubble that used to be a hangar was being hauled away by a line of trucks.

Merlin engines hummed as a quartet of humpbacked Hurricane fighters bounced, then lifted into the air. They watched the fighters climb into scattered clouds.

"Off on patrol," Sean said.

"I imagine." Sharon looked east. *I don't like being in the open like this.*

"Don't worry. No reports yet of the Luftwaffe bombers building up over France. Today they're sending their fighters over to see if they can lure our boys up for a fight."

Sharon turned.

"Hello, William," Sean said.

"I hear you've had quite an adventure." William wiped his hands with a rag that might have been white at one time. There were dark half-moon smudges under his eyes.

"Been working around the clock?" Sharon asked.

William nodded. "The losses from yesterday had to be replaced. There have been people looking for you." He pointed at Sharon.

"The ATA?" Sharon asked.

"An ATA pilot or two, and some fellows in black suits." William watched the sky behind Sharon.

"What do you see?" Sharon turned to watch.

A camouflaged Anson was on finals. The wings rocked and the engines roared.

Sharon recognized the questionable piloting skills. "Roger." She put her hand on Sean's shoulder. *Christ, I hope the asshole's not drunk.*

"The drunkard." Sean and William said it at the same time. They looked at one another and laughed.

By the time they were through laughing, the Anson was taxiing their way.

"Better stand over here." William indicated the corner of the hangar. "This git's famous for running into anything and everything." Sean led the way as they kept the hangar between them and the approaching air taxi.

"You taking Sean with you?" William asked.

Sharon nodded as the Anson's Cheetah engines roared.

"Patrick would approve!" William said over the sound of the engines.

Sharon looked at her brother and felt a fistful of grief rising up inside. *Hold on. Now all we have to do is get Roger to go along with taking Sean on this trip.*

One after the other, the Anson's engines shut down. Roger clambered out of the aircraft. He stepped off the wing and onto the ground. He rubbed his shin. "Bloody crate! I'm forever smashing my leg against that bloody spar!" Roger turned to face them. "Where the fuck have you been? Mother's been nagging me like an old hen to find you and bring you home."

"Well, we're here, and ready to fly back to White Waltham." Sharon smiled at Sean.

"We? Mother said nothin' about we. He said to bring you back. Not you and some boy. I'm not a bloody school bus driver hauling kids around the country! Besides, I'm only authorized to fly ATA personnel." Roger wiped the back of his hand across his mouth.

Sharon closed her eyes. "Asshole."

"What did she call me?" Roger looked at William for confirmation.

William gave Sharon a warning glance, then turned to Roger. "Come on. I've been told to hand something over to you. It's in the office at the back of the hangar. It'll cure whatever ails you."

"What did you call me?" Roger turned to Sharon.

William took Roger around the shoulders and aimed him into the hangar. "Come along with me, old boy. A wee taste of the rum will set you right." William looked over his shoulder and cocked his head in the direction of the Anson.

"Ever have a ride in one of these before?" Sharon asked.

"Of course. Not my favourite, though. Winding up and down the undercarriage is a bloody chore." Sean approached the Anson. "Should we do a walk around first?"

Sharon followed. *Where have I heard this before? He sounds just like me at his age.*

"How many times have you gone flying?" Sharon watched as he ducked under a wing and checked the range of motion in the aileron.

Sean shrugged. "Don't know. Plenty, as my dad used to say."

"How often did you come here?" Sharon followed along as Sean picked all of the right spots for a preflight inspection.

"After school. Weekends." Sean moved to the landing gear.

*He's just the right size for checking under this aircraft.* Sharon bent at the waist to follow him. Her hand rubbed the underside of the wing so she wouldn't bump her head on one thing or another.

Sean completed the check, then opened the door near the trailing edge of the wing.

Sharon followed him inside into the cockpit. It felt like a greenhouse and smelled of oil, dust, cigarette smoke, old booze, and body odour. "You sure know your way around the Anson."

Sean turned. There were tears in his eyes. "My dad taught me. Said I'd make a good pilot if I decided that's what I wanted."

"Did your mom ever go along for the ride?" Sharon squeezed past Sean and into the pilot's seat.

Sean sat in the next seat. He shook his head. "She hated flying. Always made her sick." He looked at the fuel cocks. "Roger had it all wrong."

Sharon looked at the fuel indicators. One was off and the other set to draw fuel from the outer tank. "If he didn't notice, he would have starved the engines of fuel." Sharon tapped the port fuel gauge. It was on empty. "Good work, Sean." She selected inner tanks from both wings where the gauges indicated the tanks were full.

"Dad thought Roger was a drunk and an accident waiting to happen." Sean looked over the edge of the cockpit and out onto the wing. "Dad said you were a good pilot."

Sharon didn't know whether to smile or cry.

"He said he liked you straight off, and that I would like you, too." Sean looked over his shoulder.

"What did your mother think of all of this? You know, me being Patrick's daughter."

"Here comes William." Sean turned to face his sister. "My mother was upset at first. Then, after a couple of days, she thought that all of this happened long before her, so she was looking forward to meeting you."

"How come you sound like a little old man?" Sharon heard the door open at the aft end of the fuselage.

"Everyone calls him the little old man." William's head and shoulders appeared at the door. "The drunken sod gulped down the better part of a bottle of rum. You want us to strap him in the back seat, or do you want to leave him in the office to sleep it off?"

"We'd better take him with us. Need some help?" Sharon asked.

William shook his head. "Got a couple of volunteers who are all too happy to see the back of Jolly Roger. Back in a bit."

Sharon turned and went through her preflight checks as she read the card on the Anson.

Sean watched her go through the routine. "Have you flown one of these before?"

"Once." Sharon reached over to Sean. "You know how to put on your safety harness?"

"Of course." Sean rolled his eyes.

"Let me see. It's my job to make sure you're secure." She smiled as she waited to see that he did it right.

Sean wiggled into his Sutton harness and secured it under his chin. "It's a little high up, but this is the best arrangement for some- one my size."

Sharon gave the harness a tug. "Looks right." She reached for her own harness.

William entered the rear of the aircraft. "Okay, you push from your end, and I'll pull from this."

Sharon turned to watch as William sat on the wing spar. He pulled Roger into the narrow fuselage.

Roger's chin rested on his chest. He seemed to take an intense in- terest in the fly of his trousers.

"Let's get you secured." William grabbed the two ends of Roger's lap belt and cinched it tight.

"Can 'ardly breathe," Roger said.

William waved away the secondhand alcohol oozing from Roger.

Sharon asked, "Is he going anywhere?"

William turned and offered his hand to Sean. "No. Roger'll be asleep before you get where you're going. Sean, take care of yourself." He cocked his head in Sharon's direction. "Your sister's more than a fair pilot. And just between you, me, and the wind, she's an ace. Seen the proof myself." He clambered down the fuselage and squeezed out the door. He pounded on it after he secured it.

Sharon turned around.

"An ace?" Sean studied her as she pulled on her flying helmet.

Sharon spotted William at the nose of the Anson. She leaned closer to the open side window. "Clear!"

William nodded.

She started the first engine, then the second.

William waved as they taxied out to the runway.

Sean watched Sharon's every move and pulled himself up to peer out the canopy window when she opened the throttles for takeoff.

There was the familiar thrill as the wheels left the ground. They climbed and headed northwest.

When the gear was up, she looked at Sean. His head was leaning to one side and his eyes were closed.

She looked over her shoulder. Roger had his head leaning up against the fuselage. His mouth was open wide. Sharon thought, *At least I don't have to listen to him snore.*

She kept her head on a swivel as they flew along the south side of London. By using the creases in the flesh of her hands, where her fingers met her palms, she could minimize the pain from her blisters.

On the horizon, to the southwest, a black column of smoke rose and was brushed across the sky by the ocean breeze.

o **"Where the hell have you been?"** Mother stood scratching the top of his head. He leaned in the doorway of the dispersal hut. "And where the hell is Roger?"

"He's sleeping it off in the back of the Anson," Sharon said.

"Where have you been?" Mother looked at Sean.

"She dug me out," Sean said.

"This is your brother?" Mother smiled and offered his hand to the boy.

Sean rolled up his sleeve and took Mother's hand.

"And?" Mother asked.

Sharon watched his face and saw him trying to put the various bits of information together. He looked at Sharon. "How drunk is Roger?"

"Stinking," she said.

"Blotto," Sean said.

"How'd he get drunk?"

"One of the aircraftsmen helped us out — he was being obstinate."

"He what?" Mother looked at Sharon.

*I really don't care what anyone thinks. We did what was necessary. That's all that needs to be said.*

"William took him into my father's office," Sean said. "Gave him some rum while we checked out the Anson."

Mother frowned at Sharon.

"Roger wasn't going to allow me to take Sean on the aircraft. Said something about regulations. So William got him drunk, while we did a preflight," Sharon said.

"Good thing, too, because Roger had the fuel cocks all wrong." Sean crossed his arms. "And he's always in his cups, anyway. Could I please have something to eat?"

"Where are your parents?" Mother asked.

"Dead."

"We're just back from the funeral." Sharon shrugged when Mother made eye contact. She saw a shudder run through him.

"And what happened to your face and hands?"

"She dug me out after the bomber crashed into my house." Sean looked in the direction of the canteen. Pilots were gathered around, grabbing a sandwich and drinking tea. "Sharon could use a cup of coffee. She's pretty tired after all she's been through. Did you know that she's an ace?"

"I'll pretend I didn't hear that last part." Mother looked out over the airfield, then back at the main building. "The two of you need to get something to eat. I'll come and talk to you in a minute." He turned and stepped inside the main building.

"What do you think he'll do?" Sean asked.

"Don't know." They walked toward the canteen. *God, I need a cup of coffee.* Sharon caught a whiff of her stale clothes and unwashed body. *And a bath.*

"I bet we'll be in loads of trouble," Sean said.

*He sounds like he's looking forward to it.* "What else could happen?"

"What will you have?" The woman behind the counter smiled down at Sean.

"Sandwich, please," Sean said.

"Spam or Spam?" she asked.

Sean smiled.

She handed him a sandwich wrapped in waxed paper.

"Thank you." Sean opened the wrapper and bit.

"And you?" the woman asked.

"Coffee, please." Sharon took it and went outside to sit under a tree with Sean. She leaned her back up against the trunk. Her belly growled. *I don't think I could stomach Spam right now.*

o **Sharon stared at the blades of grass** in front of her face. She blinked. *Am I asleep or awake?*

"You were screaming." Sean sat across from her. He was open-mouthed and wide-eyed.

She wiped the wet from the side of her face and sat up. Every nerve in her arms and back transmitted a symphony of pain. "What time is it?" The stink of seared flesh was in her nose and the syrupy, copper taste of blood at the back of her throat — a leftover from the nightmare.

"I don't know." Sean rolled a ball of waxed paper from hand to hand. "You were screaming. Was it a nightmare?"

Sharon nodded but kept her eyes open. *Christ, don't close your eyes or the horror will return.*

"Mother has a message for you." He handed Sharon a piece of paper.

She recognized it as a blank delivery chit.

"He wrote a note on the back."

She turned it over.

GET SOME SLEEP.

THE C.O. SAYS THE BOY CAN'T STAY. TOO DANGEROUS
AROUND THE AIRFIELDS.

YOU HAVE TWO DAYS LEAVE. ONE LYSANDER
DELIVERY FIRST THING TOMORROW, AND THEN
YOU'RE OFF.

GERARD D'ERLANGER ARRIVES FRIDAY. ASKED
SPECIFICALLY TO SEE YOU AT 20:00 SHARP.

GREEN

"Let's go. I need a bath." She stood up and brushed the grass from her clothing. "How come I'm covered in this stuff?"

Sean looked away and hid his green fingers behind his back. "I had to do something while you were sleeping."

# CHAPTER 18
## [ TUESDAY, AUGUST 20, 1940 ]

**Sharon stood at the front door of Linda's place,** or at least the home her aunt had loaned them. "Come on! Sean, we have to hurry."

Sean stood at the top of the stairs, buttoning his shirt. "What about breakfast?"

"We'll grab a bite at the canteen. We've got to catch the air taxi. It's leaving in fifteen minutes!" She slapped the green canvas bag against her thigh for effect. *Did I remember my lipstick?* She reached inside to check.

"Will it be Roger again?" Sean clumped down the stairs.

"I don't know." Sharon pulled the keys out of her pocket.

Sean pushed past her and out the door. "He won't let me on the plane."

*We need to get you some new clothes.* And *we need to talk with someone about keeping us together.*

She closed the door, locked it, and ran past Sean as he tied one of his shoelaces. "Come on!"

Forty-five minutes later, they stood at a hangar somewhere north of London where a newly minted Lysander, with undersurfaces painted black and uppers in green and grey, stuck its round nose out into the rain.

"Never had a ride in a Lizzie," Sean said as they ducked inside the hangar. It smelled of oil, mice, dope, and gasoline.

"Just had her test flight yesterday, and she's all ready to go. Got some instructions for you right here." The mechanic tapped the breast pocket of his grey coveralls. He pulled the envelope out and handed it to Sharon. His fingernails were black, and he left oily fingerprints on the paper. "The young lad going for a ride with you?"

"Yes." Sharon opened the envelope and found a note inside. "Pick up a passenger at Gibraltar Farm." She folded the note and stashed it in her bag. *It's Tempsford again. I wonder what will be waiting for us there?* "Come on, Sean, let's do the walk around."

She reached into her bag, pulled out her lipstick, and applied a fresh layer of red. *I wonder if Michael will be there.*

With Sean safely stowed in the observer's seat behind her, Sharon concentrated on getting them off the soggy runway and into the air.

After they were airborne, Sharon checked over her shoulder and saw Sean asleep, his head leaning against one side of the canopy.

She eased the aircraft up against the belly of the solid overcast. *That way, Jerry can't attack us from above. I can get us into cloud at the first sign of trouble.* That's the way she flew north to Tempsford.

After landing, she taxied up to the newly-constructed hangar. The workers were inside, finishing up the interior of the building. *That was fast,* Sharon thought.

The three-blade propeller slowed and stopped. She double-checked to make sure the switches were off before she undid her harness and turned around. Sean slept with his chin on his chest. His shirt collar was tucked up under his ears, and he looked at peace despite what had happened in the past couple of days.

Sharon slid the canopy back and rain pelted down on her. She climbed down the side and onto the undercarriage strut. *How am I going to get him out of there?*

"Come on, help me swing the tail around." She turned and saw Michael standing under the wing.

"Will you ever stop doing that?" Sharon asked.

"Doing what?"

"Sneaking up on me."

"Oh, that." Michael smiled. "It's expected behaviour, given my present occupation."

"I've got my brother with me."

"Brother?" Michael tilted his head to one side and stared at her.

"My father is dead. Sean's mother is dead. I — we — had to dig Sean out." Sharon held out her blistered hands. "He's my brother." *Christ, why am I so tongue-tied and nearly bloody incoherent around this man?*

Michael thought for a moment. "The Lysander is supposed to be delivered by Friday, noon. You've got a forty-eight-hour pass."

"How did you know I had a pass?" Sharon asked.

Michael shrugged. "Sometimes it's best not to ask too many questions. Do you mind if we drop in on Honeysuckle and Linda?"

"Where are they?" Sharon asked.

"At home." Michael stuck his hands in his pockets. "It's cold out here."

"Are you coming with us?" Sharon asked.

Michael nodded. "Are you going to help me swing the tail around?"

"Where are you going to sit?" Sharon grabbed one side of the tail plane as Michael lifted the other.

"I'll find a spot next to Sean. You forget I've ridden in one of these before. You did say his name is Sean, right?"

They lifted the tail and swung the Lysander 180 degrees.

"Yes."

"You dug him out, then?"

Sharon shrugged and nodded.

They set the tail down.

"Where are we going?" Sharon asked.

"Home, of course. My home. You're expected. Are you going to answer my question?" Michael climbed the ladder up the side of the Lysander.

Sharon climbed up into the cockpit and closed the canopy. "We'll have to refuel on the way." She began her preflight check.

Michael slid back the rear canopy. "They're expecting us to refuel in Leeds. We're in your hands." He swung his legs inside, gingerly easing himself next to Sean.

"Really. Is there anything you haven't thought of, Michael?"

"The weather. I hadn't thought the weather would be this dreadful." He slid the rear canopy closed.

*Thankfully, the overcast is still at one thousand feet, or we might have to turn back.* Sharon did a mental calculation for a heading that would take them to Leeds.

She took off and headed northwest.

The responsibility of having two passengers weighed on her. She scanned the sky constantly. Over her shoulders, she caught glimpses of Michael propping Sean up so that her brother's head wouldn't bump against the canopy or any one of the annoying bits of metal that could do some damage. She smiled at the two of them. *Michael can make me smile even at the worst of times.*

When she landed at Leeds, while she supervised the refueling, she saw Michael and Sean in conversation. Sean smiled and laughed. Sharon felt something close to joy.

After takeoff, she followed the A65 northwest. She kept the wet black ribbon of tarmac to her left while she concentrated on what might be ahead. She looked at her altimeter: eight hundred feet. They were down to five hundred when she spotted Lacey Hall and the Townsend farm nearby.

She eased back on the throttle and lowered the flaps. Sharon took a good look at the pasture running north-south on the far side of the farm buildings.

She turned downwind and did her checks. The Lysander slowed to ninety-five knots. On finals, she flared at seventy-five knots, kept the power on, eased them onto the grass, pulled back on the stick, cut the power, and applied the brakes. Even on the wet grass, they landed well short of the rock wall and the gate leading to Honeysuckle's garden.

After shutting down, Sharon watched the boys climb out the back. Sean stood under the wing and gave her the thumbs up. Michael stood next to him and waited.

Sharon watched them for a moment. *Those two look good together. How did I end up with two men in my life?*

She slid open the canopy and felt her way down the slick side of the fuselage. After closing the canopy, she dropped to the ground.

"And who is this?" Honeysuckle stood there in her slacks and jacket, as well as a pair of Wellington boots and an umbrella. She looked at Sharon.

"Sean, this is Honeysuckle. Sean is my brother." Sharon smiled at the boy.

"Of course he is." Honeysuckle walked over to Sean and wrapped her arm around his shoulder. "Dinner is almost ready. Are you hungry?"

*Honeysuckle doesn't appear to be surprised in the least.*

Michael and Sharon followed along behind. He caught up to her, touched her hand and she squeezed his.

Near the house, Sean said something to Honeysuckle and she leaned down to listen. The wind carried Honeysuckle's voice. "I'm not at all surprised. Your sister really is a fierce one."

o **"What happened to your hands?"** Linda sat at the head of the kitchen table. The remains of a ham, fresh potatoes, peas, and bread were still spread over the surface.

Sharon used her fingers to strip a piece of meat from the ham.

"She dug me out," Sean said.

"What?" Linda sat with her legs propped up on a kitchen chair and looked at her friend.

"I was hoping someone would tell us the story." Michael frowned in Sharon's general direction.

"A Dornier hit my house. I hid under the table. Sharon and Nigel dug all night and got me out." Sean lifted his cup of milk, took a drink, and wiped away the moustache.

*Change the subject.* "How are your legs healing?"

"Better. I have to go back in a month for another checkup and there will be more skin grafts. How is the flying going?" Linda adjusted one of her legs by lifting the fabric on her flannel bottoms.

Honeysuckle sat at the other end of the table, her chin leaning on her interlocking fingers. Her eyes appeared half closed.

Michael leaned back. The chair complained. He turned his head to watch Sharon.

Sharon said, "Things are pretty hectic. More deliveries going to forward airfields. Some hush-hush deliveries." She glanced at Michael as she reached for her coffee.

Honeysuckle lifted her chin off of her fingers. "We're hearing rumours that you're an ace."

Sharon looked at Sean. "So that's what you two were talking about."

Sean's face turned red.

"He's proud of you," Honeysuckle said.

Linda said, "Details. Don't you dare leave out a thing."

Sharon told them the story from start to finish. She wept as she told them about what happened to her father, and she wept as she told them about landing a damaged Spitfire with the remains of the Luftwaffe pilot on the chin of the fuselage.

"My god, it's true," Michael said.

"What's true?" Sharon asked.

Linda said, "When you went missing after the attack on Biggin Hill, Michael was frantic. He found out as much as he could. One unconfirmed report described a female pilot who was reported to have shot down five aircraft. Michael even went so far as to check the map for five wreckage sites that were outside of the area of reported and confirmed kills of enemy aircraft." Linda shifted her weight to get her legs on the floor. She winced with the pain.

Sean looked at Honeysuckle. "I told you she was an ace."

Michael looked at his hands as he rubbed them together. "We need to have counts of downed aircraft for a variety of reasons. One is so that we can keep an accurate record of the numbers of German bombers and fighters shot down. Another is so that we can inspect the wreckage for evidence of any specialized equipment being used by the Luftwaffe."

"So you work for the SOE." Sharon looked at Michael.

Michael frowned.

"He has a very specialized job," Honeysuckle said.

Linda reached across the table to touch Sharon's hands. "Do you want some medicine for those?"

"They're better today." *It just feels good to be here with you again.*

Honeysuckle asked, "And what about Sean? He'll stay here with me, of course. He'll be safe."

Sean looked at his sister.

Sharon lifted her hands. "I. . ."

Sean began to weep. "You're leaving me, too?"

"I. . ." Sharon said.

Sean stood up. His chair fell over onto its back. "You can't leave me! There's no one else!" He smashed his fists onto the table. The china and cutlery rattled.

Michael stood up. "Come on, Sean. Let's you and I go into the sitting room."

Sean pointed at his sister. "I'm not going anywhere unless she's there!"

Linda asked, "What makes you think she won't be coming here to see you any chance she gets? She needs to know you're safe, so she can keep doing her job."

# CHAPTER 19
## [ WEDNESDAY, AUGUST 21, 1940 ]

*"I was thinking I should visit Mr. McGregor this morning."*
Sharon sat across from Honeysuckle and next to Linda at the kitchen table.

"Why?" Linda put her elbows on the table.

"Linda, just let her alone." Honeysuckle glared at her daughter. "Why are you trying to provoke her?"

"I need to consider what happens to Sean," Sharon said. "I have to think about him and what he needs." *What's Linda's problem?*

"What did you really want to say?" Linda pointed her teaspoon at Sharon. "I mean, you haven't been yourself since you got here. What is the matter with you?"

"Piss off!" Sharon said.

Linda put her spoon down and sat back. "There's the girl I know and love! That must feel better. You're getting your feistiness back. When you walked in the door, you looked like a whipped dog."

"You were just playing with me! Trying to provoke me!" Sharon almost smiled.

"That's right." Linda pointed her finger at her friend. "Everything you've done these past weeks, you've had to do. It's very simple: it's the way things are right now."

"My father died right in front of me. He was alive, and then he was dead. So I went after the bastards! I must have killed at least fifteen of them. And if you add that total to the others, I've killed over twenty people! I'm a murderer!" Sharon wiped the tears from her cheeks.

Honeysuckle looked from her daughter to Sharon and back again.

"I don't want to be a killer! Look at these hands! They're the hands of a killer." She held out her bruised, blistered, and scratched hands.

"In case the three of you haven't noticed, there's a war on, and before it's over, plenty more of us will have blood on our hands." Michael sat down next to Sharon. He put his arm around her shoulders.

He smelled of soap and shampoo. *He smells awfully good.* She looked at the open neck of his shirt, then leaned into him.

She pulled McGregor's business card out of her breast pocket. "Is there any way I could get a lift into Ilkley to see Walter McGregor?"

Michael smiled. "I'm sure something could be arranged. Walter always likes a visit, especially if that visitor is a female."

Sharon felt herself blushing.

"I'm coming, too!" Sean stood in the doorway.

"Of course you are," Michael said.

"And I should say hello to my grandmother," Sharon said.

Silence was an unpleasant visitor at the breakfast table.

Sharon looked at each of them. "What's happened?"

Honeysuckle put her cup down. "We haven't seen your grandmother since the last time you saw her."

"What's that mean?" Sharon asked.

Sean sat down beside her. "You have a grandmother?"

Linda leaned her elbows on the table. "It means your uncle is keeping her at home. She's being encouraged to stay away from us. It's nothing new, really. When your grandfather was alive, we often wouldn't see her for months on end."

Sharon looked out the window and remembered her mother talking about her home in England when Leslie had said, "Living there, I felt like a prisoner. Here, I feel free."

"What are you thinking?" Honeysuckle asked.

"Something my mother said about her brother and father and how they were obsessed with money, position, and their reputations. That Cornelia was like a possession to her father. Leslie was happy she'd taken me to Canada." Sharon looked at Sean. "I'm just beginning to understand why she never wanted to come back and visit her family."

"Do you still want to go to Ilkley?" Linda asked.

"More than ever." Sharon drained her coffee.

Honeysuckle looked at Sean. "Would you like something to eat before you go?"

Sean blushed.

No one laughed, but when Sharon looked around the table, all were smiling.

o **Walter McGregor's office was much like his hair** — a bit tangled and unruly. "Let me find you a seat." He lifted a file off of a leather chair and indicated that Sharon should sit down.

"Thank you for seeing me on such short notice." Sharon sat and crossed her legs.

"A pleasure, I can assure you." He sat down. He peered back at her from between two stacks of files.

"You said you would represent me?" Sharon looked out the window. *I wonder how long Sean will last, sitting in the car.* She remembered Sean's panicked appeals when Michael dropped her off in front of McGregor's office.

"Yes, I did." McGregor leaned back in his chair.

"I would like to name a beneficiary, should something happen to me." Sharon looked at her hands and interlocked the fingers to keep them still.

"Who would this be?" Walter asked.

"My brother. Half-brother, really. My father's son." *I must sound like an idiot.*

"First, we'll have to establish that you are your mother's heir. Do you have any documents, like a birth certificate? I'll also need your mother's death certificate."

Sharon nodded. "I brought them all with me. My mother insisted

I keep a file of papers. It's just that they're in White Waltham right now." *Why didn't I think to bring them here?*

"Would you be able to mail them to me?" Walter asked.

Sharon nodded. "Yes."

"And would you like me to begin proceedings to establish that you are the legal heir to your mother's portion of the estate?"

*I wonder how my grandmother will react to this?* "Yes."

"If you can come back in an hour, I will have documents ready for you to sign. Then I will proceed with establishing you as Leslie's heir, after I receive the documents in the mail." Walter rubbed two freckled hands together.

"You seem pleased."

Walter smiled. "Actually, I've been waiting for someone to come along so that I could take on Marmaduke."

"Don't I have to pay you?"

Walter's smile broadened. "It just so happens that I am retained by your family. In effect, your uncle is paying me to help you. At least for now."

"So you'll be in contact?"

"I will. You will supply a mailing address with your documents?"

"Yes, of course." *That might be difficult, the way I move around.*

Walter stood up and offered his hand. She shook it and winced. Walter cocked his head to one side and looked at her thoughtfully. "I'll see you in an hour, then."

Sean and Michael were waiting outside in the car.

Sharon opened her door. "He wants me back in an hour to sign some papers."

"Should be just enough time," Michael said.

"Just enough time for what?" Sharon asked.

"To see the Cow and Calf rocks." Sean made it sound like she should have already known what their plans were.

They took a road up a hill, then hiked along a trail through a pasture green from the rain. A rocky sandstone outcrop sat at the top of the hill. One boulder had fallen and was tilted at an angle away from the others.

"Can we climb there?" Sean asked.

"I don't know." Sharon looked at the height of the outcrop and the sheer drop on this side.

"It's easier and quite safe around the back. The view is spectacular. Especially on a cloudy day with shafts of sunlight shining through." Michael parked and waited for Sharon's decision.

Sean looked down over the valley.

"As long as we're careful." Sharon followed Sean, who trailed Michael around to the back of the boulders.

They made it to the top, and Sharon held Sean back from the edge. Shafts of sunlight streamed down through the clouds and illuminated the valley and the town. "It's beautiful," she said.

Sharon recalled a summer day in the foothills of Alberta. Her mother would drive southwest of the city to where a massive pair of boulders the size of mansions had been deposited in a field. Mother and daughter often spent half a day there, eating a picnic lunch, talking, and enjoying the view. Sharon had scrambled over the rocks with the mountains behind her and the prairies spread out in front.

Today, she could see her mother there, smiling, her hand shading her eyes as she told her daughter to take care as she climbed, all the while explaining to Sharon that there were rocks like this near where she'd grown up in England.

"Thank you." Sharon tucked her arm inside Michael's elbow.

Michael leaned closer. "Your brother thinks the world of you."

"I think the world of him. That's why I need to know he'll be safe and looked after, no matter what happens to me."

Michael watched Sean as he stood and looked out over the valley. "You need to be forewarned about your Uncle Marmaduke. He is very well informed. By the time we get back to my mother's farm, he will have heard that you met with Mr. McGregor."

"McGregor will tell him?" *I've trusted the wrong person for a lawyer.*

Michael shook his head. "Many of the people in the town and surrounding countryside still live very traditional lives. Marmaduke Lacey is lord of the manor, a member of the privileged class; a man with power. Someone will report you to Marmaduke in the hope of getting in his good graces. McGregor is not one of them."

"Out of the frying pan and into the fire." Sharon took a deep breath.

"Not exactly. If you understand your enemy, then you will adopt appropriate tactics."

Sharon frowned.

"Marmaduke will most likely send someone over to do a reconnoiter at our home. Expect the visit and be prepared. It's quite simple, actually. It's also important to understand that you have an advantage." Michael looked at his watch.

"What's that?" Sharon asked.

"You're a Canadian. You don't know the rules that he expects you to play by. You will be unpredictable. And, I believe, you are not afraid of the man. Most who know him are. Finally, he underestimates you because you are, in his mind, nothing more than a woman. He believes you to be his inferior in breeding and in intellect, which gives you another advantage." Michael waved Sean over. "We need to start back."

o *Walter McGregor said, "That's all I require."* He gathered up the signed papers and put them in a file folder. "Please send me the remaining documents, and I'll begin work from this end." He offered his hand. "A pleasure to see you again."

Sharon shook his hand. *I wonder how close he was to my mother?*

Michael drove them back to meet Honeysuckle and Linda for lunch.

In the middle of the meal, there was a polite knock on the door. Sharon set down her spoon and looked at Michael.

"Who would that be, I wonder?" Honeysuckle winked at her son.

He nodded, stood, and disappeared down the hallway to the front door. "Hello, Cornelia, what a pleasant surprise."

"Oh Michael, I hope I'm not interrupting," Cornelia said.

"Not at all. Join us for some tea," Michael said.

There was the sound of footsteps, and then Cornelia stood before them. She looked from face to face and settled on Sharon. "Oh, I hoped it was you who'd flown in. I've been expecting you to drop by for a visit."

Sharon sat up straight. *Breathe and just say whatever you want to say.*

"Sit down, dear," Honeysuckle said.

"Your Uncle Marmaduke would like to see his niece again." Cornelia sat down next to Linda. "And how are you feeling?" She patted Linda's leg.

Linda winced with pain. "Better."

"My Uncle Marmaduke was extremely inappropriate with me the last time we met," Sharon said. "I'm really not interested in repeating the experience with him. It's good to see you, though." Sharon put a slice of leftover ham in her mouth. *I've said too much!*

"Oh, I'm sure you're mistaken." Cornelia looked around the table for support. "Your uncle is a very affectionate man."

Linda choked and Michael made a show of patting her on the back.

Sharon put her hand over her mouth. "My mother always spoke well of you, Grandmother. I always wondered why she never mentioned her brother. Now I think I know why."

Cornelia's eyes narrowed and focused on Sean. "And who is this?"

"Sean. My brother."

There was a collective intake of breath around the table. Cornelia became intensely interested in the way Honeysuckle was pouring her a cup of tea. "From Canada?" she asked.

"Where were you born, Sean?" Sharon asked.

Cornelia looked at Sharon as if to say, *You don't know?*

"London," Sean said.

"That's nice." Cornelia stared out the window, then back to Sharon. "And what have you been up to these last few days?"

"Oh, you know, there's a war on. . . . I've been learning how to kill."

o **"I don't want you to go."** Sean stood before Sharon, looking at his toes with his hands in his pockets.

Everyone was in the sitting room after supper.

"Sean, if I don't go, the Royal Air Force won't get their fighters. And if the fighters don't go up to stop the Luftwaffe, then Hitler will invade. I have to go. Then you can be safe, and I need to know that you will be safe." Sharon felt anxiety telegraphing shivers to her fingertips. She turned to Honeysuckle. "I'm sorry about this."

"May I interject?" Honeysuckle asked.

"Go right ahead," Sharon said.

Linda smiled.

Michael studied Sean's reactions.

Honeysuckle motioned with her hand for Sean to sit between her and Sharon. Sean sat down reluctantly and crossed his arms in front of his chest.

"And you can see that I'm running the farm mostly by myself, can't you?" Honeysuckle asked.

Sean stared back at her.

"You can see that Linda has been injured — burned, actually. Did you know that it was your sister who got Linda to the hospital for burn victims?"

"No," Sean said.

"The surgeon thinks that Sharon saved my legs by getting me there right away," Linda said. "I may have to endure more operations, but I'm beginning to heal because of your sister."

"I just want to be with Sharon," Sean said.

"The point is that because of the war, you need to be away from the places most likely to be attacked. I need help on the farm. Sharon needs to know that you're safe." Honeysuckle leaned away from Sean to better gauge his reactions.

"She's right. I need to know that you're okay." Sharon combed her fingers through his hair.

"When you pulled me out from under the table, I thought you weren't going to leave. There's no one else, you know." Sean wiped his eyes with the back of his right hand.

"She's here now, and she'll be here every leave she gets," Linda said. "And when I have to go back to East Grinstead for another operation, you will accompany me so we can visit her. The nice thing about the hospital is that it's close to White Waltham, where Sharon is based."

Sean looked at his sister. "That's true?"

Sharon nodded.

"Can you keep a secret?" Michael asked.

Sean looked at him.

"Can you all keep a secret?" Michael looked around the room.

"Yes, Michael, we can," Honeysuckle said.

"Hitler is massing an invasion fleet in France. He's given Goering, the man in charge of the Luftwaffe, the job of defeating the RAF. If the RAF can hold off the Luftwaffe, then Hitler cannot invade. What Sharon is doing right now is crucial. We need every pilot and we need every aircraft to stop the Luftwaffe. Sean, Sharon and I need you here to make sure that Linda and Honeysuckle are safe." Michael glanced at Sharon.

"I won't tell anyone about the invasion force," Sean said.

"And Sharon will promise to keep her eyes open and stay away from the air battles," Michael said.

"I promise," Sharon said.

"And you'll come back and visit us every time you have leave?" Honeysuckle asked.

"You won't be able to keep me away." Sharon began to cry. She wiped at her face.

"What's the matter?" Sean asked.

Sharon shook her head because she found she could no longer speak.

# CHAPTER 20
## [ THURSDAY, AUGUST 22, 1940 ]

**Sharon and Michael landed at Tempsford** right after a squall. Rain puddled on the runway and the concrete apron out front of the new hangar.

Two men wearing leather vests guided them to the mouth of the hangar. Sharon shut down, and the men pushed the Lysander inside. The tires sighed over the shiny concrete surface, and the engine ticked as it cooled.

Sharon climbed down the side and grabbed the tail to swing it around. Michael stood beside her and helped her by lifting the horizontal stabilizer.

One of the mechanics said, "We need to get busy on this one. It needs a long-range fuel tank." Then he went to grab his tools.

"My car is around the corner. I'll give you a lift into Bedford." Michael walked out of the hangar.

Sharon reached into her bag, applied a fresh coat of lipstick, and followed.

Michael squeezed into the car and started it. The red MG's convertible top was up. "Hop in."

Sharon opened the door and ducked low. *You have to be a bloody contortionist to get into this thing.*

"Sorry, it's a bit cramped." He drove off in the direction of Bedford.

Sharon recognized the route this time. *Why is he driving slower?*

"Sean will be fine. I think Mother is excited to have someone around. She hasn't known what to do with herself with all of us away and her having to run the place on her own." Michael downshifted as they reached the outskirts of a town.

"I don't know how to thank her — well, all of you, actually. I feel I've asked too much of your mother." Sharon found herself comfortably close to Michael. He had an unruly bit of sandy blond hair at the side of his head. She wanted to push it back into place, couldn't think of a plausible excuse for touching him, so did it anyway. He smiled.

"You have to understand, we're the ones who are grateful, after what you did for Linda. It's the least we can do. Besides, Sean is a fine chap. Still, I do have a favour to ask." Michael looked sideways at her.

"What is it?"

"Take Linda up for a ride the next time you have your hands on an aircraft at the farm. I think she wants to go, but is afraid."

"Afraid to ask?"

"No, afraid to get back on the horse that threw her, as they say." Michael shifted into a higher gear.

*And, as they say, why am I always delivering Lysanders to Tempsford when you're there?* "I'll see if I can coax her. How many more operations will she need?"

Michael put both hands on the wheel. "I don't know. Much of the work that's being done at East Grinstead is revolutionary, if you go by the name the patients call themselves."

"You mean the guinea pigs?"

"Exactly. All I know is that it appears to be working, and she won't lose her legs to infection." Michael looked sideways at her. "Thanks to you."

"You were very kind to Sean."

"He's a wonderful fellow." Michael smiled. "And very proud of you. He told me all about you pulling him out of the rubble."

"They told me he was dead. I thought we were recovering his body."
Sharon looked ahead and saw four aircraft skimming overtop the rolling countryside.

"Hurricanes?" Michael asked.

"Messerschmitts."

"You're joking!"

"I'm not. Look at the way they fly. Luftwaffe tactics are different from ours. Looser formations. And those fighters have a more angular look." Sharon looked down to see that her fists were clenched and knuckles turning white.

"Then it must be true."

"What's that?" Sharon turned to him as they began to slow at the outskirts of Bedford.

"That you're a natural. That's why you were able to shoot those aircraft down. And that's why you outflew that Me. 110 pilot and broke up the bomber formation."

"How do you know so much about me? It's not common knowledge." Sharon shook her head.

"I work with some people who are in the business of finding out what's actually happening — not the daily tallies printed in the newspapers." It began to rain. Michael turned on the wipers. "I have to be careful how I say this. And, you understand, we have an Official Secrets Act." Michael eased past a horse and cart with the driver hunched under his hat and slicker. "You see, if a country is in danger of being invaded, it needs to gather information about its enemy."

Sharon leaned against her door. "I don't quite see how that allows you to know so much about me."

"Just one of the perks of my job, I suppose." Michael smiled at her.

"One of the perks of mine is that I have nightmares about the men I've killed." Sharon looked out her window.

"So do I."

Sharon turned to face him. *You don't look like a killer.*

The MG slowed.

Sharon looked ahead to see a barricade of two erect oil drums, a horizontal stretch of timber, and rolls of barbed wire. The three men at the barricade wore faded army green and had barrel chests, which had since slipped down to curl over their belts.

Michael rolled down his window and stopped.

"Advance and be recognized!" the man with the rifle said.

"Oh, not this rubbish again," Sharon said.

"Michael Townsend. We just came from Gibraltar Farm."

The home guard stuck his red face into the open window. "We've had a report of German paratroops. Who's the woman?"

"Air Transport Auxilliary," Sharon said.

"Never heard of a woman flying for the ATA." The man with the rifle backed up and looked in the direction of the other two guards.

"Now you have." Michael reached into his breast pocket and pulled out an ID card. He held it for the guard to read.

The guard took the card and held it at arm's length. "What's it say?" He walked to the barricade and showed it to his mates.

Each took a look at the card. One eventually pulled out a pair of glasses, read the card, looked over his glasses at Michael, then said something to the man with the rifle. The guard waved them ahead. The guard with the glasses handed Michael his card back as he eased past the barricade.

"The Germans won't have a chance if they ever run into those three." Michael rolled his eyes as he glanced sideways at Sharon.

She started to laugh. "They sometimes scare me more than the Nazis."

Michael's laughter stopped. "Not if you'd seen what happened in Poland and France."

"You were there?" Sharon asked.

Michael nodded. He was quiet until they reached the airfield and stopped next to a hangar. "Don't worry about d'Erlanger. He's a good chap."

"How do you know that I have a meeting with him later today?"

"It's my job to know."

Sharon saw a deep weariness in his eyes. She smiled. *Maybe I can make him laugh.* "It gets a little annoying at times."

He smiled. "Be careful." Then he leaned over and kissed her. She closed her eyes at the unexpected pleasure of the moment. The rain tattled on the roof. An aircraft engine coughed and started up. She opened her eyes, smiled, eased out of the MG, and pulled her flight gear from behind the seat. The rain ran down the back of her neck and she dashed for the open mouth of the hangar.

o*After she flew four more deliveries,* the Anson brought Sharon and another pilot back to White Waltham at suppertime.

In the mess, she found herself alone, sitting at a table, staring at a bowl of stew and a thick slice of bread. She closed her eyes and saw Sean's face. *I wonder what he's up to at the moment?* Then she saw Michael's face, and he was smiling at something she'd said.

Sharon opened her eyes, touched her lips, then picked up her fork. She speared a piece of potato, blew the heat from it, then gingerly put it between her teeth.

"May I join you?" A man of forty or so years stood across from her. He wore a blue ATA uniform with a pair of wings stitched above a breast pocket.

Sharon put her hand in front of her mouth and chewed the hot potato. "Of course." She reached for a glass of water to cool the potato's heat.

He sat down, folded his cap, and put it on the table. "Gerard d'Erlanger."

"Sharon Lacey." She shook his hand. "Are you hungry?"

"I ate before you arrived. You look famished. Mind if we chat while you eat?"

"No, I don't mind." Sharon took a deep breath and waited.

"Please, go ahead." D'Erlanger looked around the room.

Sharon scooped up a spoonful of stew and put it in her mouth. She heard the fresh quiet that had fallen over the mess and looked around. The usual clatter of dishes, cutlery, and conversation was hushed. Two tables away, a man and a woman looked at Sharon and talked behind their hands. "Well?"

"We really should talk in an office." He looked for a room they could use.

"Just talk softly. Sound dies in this room." Sharon tore off a crust of bread and dipped it in her stew.

He leaned closer. "There are unconfirmed reports that you're an ace. That you've shot down or caused more than five German aircraft to crash."

Sharon let the bread soak up some gravy. "That's more or less correct."

"Well, is it more, or is it less? Since we're talking about numbers, how many is it?"

Sharon caught a whiff of d'Erlanger. He smelled of hair oil and pipe smoke. "Eight."

His eyebrows popped up, creating creases on his forehead. "Bombers or fighters?"

"Five bombers and three fighters." *Why is he so curious about the numbers?*

"Any Messerschmitt 109s?"

"Two." Sharon closed her eyes when a flashback splattered the bloody remains of one pilot on the chin of her Spitfire. Nausea made her head spin. She pushed the bowl away from her.

"Are you all right?"

Sharon shrugged.

"We have a bit of a problem, because you've just proved some very powerful people wrong. They thought that women were unsuited for flying fighters, let alone for aerial combat. These are the very people who have opposed having women in the ATA. They will not take kindly to having to eat their words, especially if they find out that the ATA ace is a woman." D'Erlanger waited for a response.

She looked at him. *Why are we worrying about what people might think? Isn't there a war going on? Aren't the Nazis about to invade?*

"One option is to verify your successes and call the newspapers. The other is to hush it up." He turned his hands palms up on the table.

"You want me to make the decision?" *I could really care less.*

"Well?"

"I would like to keep flying."

"And?"

*And I'm no hero.* Sharon took a long breath and looked at the wall. "I don't like being a killer. Flying is what I like to do. The rest of what we are discussing is really rather ridiculous. After all, isn't there a war on?"

"Yes, of course there is. The problem is, I have to deal with the politics and the organization, as well as meeting the needs of the ATA and the RAF."

*Well, that's your problem, isn't it?* "Do I get to keep flying?"

"What kind of ridiculous question is that? Of course you will continue flying. We need pilots, and you're damned good at what you do!"

Sharon could hear the shifting of pilots at the other tables. They'd overheard the last comment. "So I didn't break any rules?"

D'Erlanger smiled. "Of course you broke some rules. All of the rules that needed to be broken, anyway."

"I'm being difficult, aren't I?"

"A little. And I'm being a bit of a Colonel Blimp."

Sharon laughed.

D'Erlanger smiled. "We'll meet again after this is over."

"What do you mean?"

"The battle. We're in the middle of it. The Luftwaffe will throw everything it has at us now."

"Oh, that battle." Sharon tried to smile but failed.

# CHAPTER 21
## [ MONDAY, AUGUST 26, 1940 ]

**"Did you hear the news?** Manston has closed down. Too much damage to the airfield and buildings. It's no wonder. It's so close to the coast that the Luftwaffe hit them with very little warning. London was bombed. So the RAF bombed Berlin last night." Mother sipped a cup of tea as Sharon wrapped her fingers around her coffee.

"So d'Erlanger was right. The Luftwaffe is throwing everything it has at us." Sharon looked at the chit in her hand.

"Do you really want to go back there?"

"I have to go sometime." Sharon folded the chit and stuffed it into the breast pocket of her blouse. She looked toward the runway, where the air taxi — a twin-engined biplane — elegantly touched down. Sharon leaned away from the wall. "My ride is here."

"See you when you get back."

An hour later, she was strapped into the cockpit of a Spitfire at Castle Bromwich. It smelled of fresh paint. *I love that new airplane smell.* Sharon leaned to the right and poked her head out of the open cockpit. "Clear!"

The aircraftsman gave her the thumbs up.

The propeller turned over and black smoke puffed out of the exhausts. The engine crackled to life.

After she took off and the wheels were tucked into the wings, Sharon scanned the sky. *I used to love this part — now I keep waiting for the Luftwaffe to pounce.*

The clouds above her gave the ground a mottled look as the fields were alternatively glittering and cast into shadow.

Sharon landed at Biggin Hill at 10:45 that morning.

She looked for William, but did not see him. She shut down and climbed off the wing as fighters took off. The air raid siren wailed.

The first wave of bombers appeared.

A big gun opened up on the other side of the field.

There was a nearby slit trench in front of a pair of anti-aircraft guns. Sharon ran to it and jumped in.

"Christ!"

She'd landed on a mechanic. "Sorry." Sharon rolled off the man.

"Oi, Freddy, it's O'Malley's daughter!"

Freddy sat up and stared at Sharon. "You're right, Bill." He held out his hand.

Sharon took his hand and shook it. "Nice to meet you."

The first bomb exploded. The ground shook. The nearby anti-aircraft guns opened up.

Sharon peeked over the rim of the trench. At the nearest gun, two people sat at the back of the Bofors. A man loaded rounds. On one side, a tiny woman wearing a too-large helmet pressed a pedal to fire the anti-aircraft shells. Two other men worked furiously bringing ammunition.

Sharon watched the way the woman concentrated, aimed, stuck her tongue out the side of her mouth, and fired.

One of the men slapped her on the helmet. "We got another one of the bastards, Annie!"

The blow almost knocked Annie off her perch; she weighed perhaps one hundred pounds. Annie pressed the pedal, stuck out her tongue, and fired again.

Sharon looked up. A Junkers 88 trailed smoke and turned for home as it jettisoned its bombs.

Thirty minutes later, Sharon met Annie at the canteen. She was eating a sandwich and sipping a cup of tea while the men of her crew talked excitedly and received congratulations.

Sharon sat down at the next table and sipped her coffee. "Nice shooting, Annie."

Annie pushed back an unruly lock of blonde hair and focused on Sharon. "Thank you, Canada." Then her blue eyes widened. "It's you! The ace!"

Conversation stopped.

"Look boys, it's the Lady Ace." Annie smiled at Sharon. "What's your name?"

"Sharon." She looked around for an escape.

"William showed us your Spitfire after the Luftwaffe gave us a pasting. How did you manage to get that wreck home?" Annie turned to face Sharon to take the measure of her.

The men went back to planning how they were going to bag their next Hun.

Annie grabbed her sandwich and tea. She came to sit next to Sharon.

"Where did you learn to shoot?" Sharon asked.

"Oh, training. You know, I was always good at that sort of thing. Throwing rocks. Slingshots. Never fired a gun before sitting on the Bofors, but I usually hit what I'm aiming at." Annie took a bite of sandwich. "You learned to fly in Canada?"

Sharon nodded. "A friend of the family taught me, and when I came over here, I heard the ATA was looking for pilots."

Laughter from the next table temporarily filled the tent.

"They're pretty full of themselves today." Annie finished off her sandwich. "God, I hope the war will be over soon. I'm sick and tired of bully beef and mutton."

"It is decidedly disgusting." Sharon looked at her sandwich, pulled off a bit of crust, and put it in her mouth. "Beef never tasted like this where I come from."

"What brought you to England?"

"Family." Sharon washed the bread down with coffee. "How did you come to be a gunner?"

Annie reached into her bag, rummaged inside, and pulled out her lipstick. She lifted a round mirror our of her side pocket and applied a bright shade of red. "My daughter, Linda. She's just three. You know, I thought I'd do my bit so that she'd be safe from Hitler and his gang. How about you, love? Who are you taking care of?"

"Sean, my brother." *I hope he got the letters I wrote last week.*

"O'Malley's son?" Annie touched Sharon's forearm.

Sharon nodded. She felt her eyes filling with tears.

"Bloody war plays hell with families."

# CHAPTER 22
## [ THURSDAY, AUGUST 29, 1940 ]

***Sharon felt absolutely knackered*** as she sagged into the wing-backed chair that took up much of the sitting room. She loosened the towel wrapped turban-like around her head and began rubbing her hair dry. She looked at the letters staring back at her from the ottoman. It was the same unnaturally hideous floral print she was sitting on. "I'd better get through these before I go to bed." She opened Sean's letter first.

DEAR SHARON,

HONEYSUCKLE SAYS I HAVE TO WRITE YOU A LETTER EVERY DAY. SAYS IT'S PART OF MY EDUCATION.

LINDA SAYS I HAVE TO WRITE YOU EVERY DAY BECAUSE YOU'RE MY SISTER, AND WE NEED TO GET ACQUAINTED (I WAS A LITTLE FOGGY ON HOW TO SPELL THAT WORD, SO SHE SPELLED IT OUT FOR ME).

LINDA SAYS YOU CAN'T GET UP HERE VERY OFTEN BECAUSE THERE IS A MAJOR BATTLE GOING ON. WELL? IS THERE A BATTLE GOING ON?

THE BBC SAYS THE NAZIS ARE ATTACKING THE AIRFIELDS, AND THAT THE RAF IS SHOOTING DOWN LOADS OF JERRIES. HAVE YOU SHOT DOWN ANY MORE? I KNOW YOU PROMISED YOU'D STAY AWAY FROM THAT, BUT I THOUGHT MAYBE YOU HAD TO DEFEND YOURSELF WHEN A SWARM OF MESSERSCHMITTS ATTACKED YOU, AND YOU HAD NO OTHER CHOICE BUT TO FIGHT FOR YOUR LIFE.

LINDA AND HONEYSUCKLE ARE WORRIED ABOUT SOMETHING. THEY
TELL ME NOTHING IS WRONG, BUT I CAN TELL. IT'S SOMETHING ABOUT
MICHAEL, BECAUSE WHEN I ASK, THEY GET TEARS IN THEIR EYES.

THIS IS MY FIRST LETTER, SO YOU SHOULD EXPECT ONE A DAY FROM
NOW ON.

YOURS TRULY,
SEAN

Sharon reached for the next letter. *Let's see what Mr. McGregor has to say.*

DEAR SHARON LACEY,

THIS LETTER IS TO INFORM YOU THAT ALL RELEVANT DOCUMENTS
HAVE ARRIVED AT THIS OFFICE.

AT THIS MOMENT, THE PROCESS WILL BEGIN TO HAVE YOU DECLARED
LESLIE LACEY'S LEGAL HEIR AND, THEREFORE, ENTITLED TO HER
INHERITANCE.

YOU WILL BE ADVISED OF FURTHER DEVELOPMENTS AS THEY OCCUR.

YOURS SINCERELY,
WALTER MCGREGOR, QC

Sharon looked at the nightstand. Her mother's letters lay there, still neatly tied with a ribbon — the letters Honeysuckle had given Sharon. She reached over and took the packet. She held them up to her nose, hoping to catch her mother's scent. Nothing.

She flipped through the letters until she got to the most recent one. She tore open the envelope, pulled out the letter, held it close to her nose, and inhaled. There was the faintest scent of her mother's lavender perfume and the musty scent of smoke from her cigarettes.

DEAR HONEYSUCKLE,

I FEAR I AM ABOUT TO IMPOSE UPON OUR FRIENDSHIP ONCE AGAIN,
AND, I BELIEVE, FOR THE LAST TIME.

I HAVE WRITTEN OFTEN AND AT GREAT LENGTH ABOUT SHARON.
BY NOW, YOU MUST FEEL AS IF YOU KNOW HER ALMOST AS WELL AS
IF SHE WERE YOUR DAUGHTER.

AFTER I AM DEAD, IT IS CLEAR TO ME THAT SHARON WILL TRAVEL TO ENGLAND TO VISIT MY FAMILY. SHE HAS ALSO EXPRESSED A DESIRE TO MEET HER FATHER. SHARON OFTEN SPOKE OF HER WISH THAT WE SHOULD VISIT ENGLAND BEFORE I BECAME ILL. SINCE THEN, SHE HAS NOT MENTIONED IT AGAIN. I AM CERTAIN THAT ONCE I AM GONE, THIS WISH WILL BRING HER TO ENGLAND, AND, I AM HOPING, TO YOUR DOORSTEP.

AS YOU ARE AWARE, A MOTHER'S MAIN WORRY IS FOR THE SAFETY OF HER CHILD. WE BOTH KNOW ABOUT THE PROCLIVITIES OF MY BROTHER, MARMADUKE. PLEASE KEEP A CLOSE WATCH ON SHARON SHOULD SHE APPEAR AT THE ESTATE. I FEAR THAT MY BROTHER'S RUTHLESS NATURE WILL GET THE BETTER OF HIM SHOULD HE MEET HER AND DISCOVER WHO SHE IS. IT IS WITH THIS IN MIND THAT I'VE ENCOURAGED HER TO VISIT YOU AND YOUR FAMILY. MY DAUGHTER, I'M AFRAID, IS THE TYPE OF PERSON WHO WILL TRAVEL OVERSEAS DESPITE THE WORSENING SITUATION IN EUROPE.

SHARON IS AN ACCOMPLISHED PILOT. YOU'VE OFTEN SPOKEN OF YOUR DAUGHTER, LINDA, AND HER PLANS TO BECOME AN AVIATRIX. PERHAPS THE PAIR OF THEM WILL FIND SOME COMMON GROUND AS A RESULT OF THIS SHARED INTEREST.

HONEYSUCKLE, YOU HAVE BEEN A DEAR FRIEND DURING MY LIFETIME AND ESPECIALLY DURING THE PAST TWENTY YEARS SINCE I LEFT ENGLAND. OVER THAT TIME, I HAVE COME TO APPRECIATE YOUR KINDNESS AND YOUR STRENGTH. BESIDES LEAVING MY DAUGHTER BEHIND, MY OTHER GREAT REGRET IS THAT I WILL BE UNABLE TO SEE YOU AGAIN.

BE ADVISED THAT I HAVE MADE ARRANGEMENTS FOR A PACKAGE TO BE DELIVERED TO YOU.

SINCERELY YOURS,
LESLIE LACEY

Sharon folded up the three letters, returned them to their envelopes, and set them on the ottoman.

# CHAPTER 23
## [ FRIDAY, AUGUST 30, 1940 ]

**"Sorry, Sharon, the commandant says** no leaves are possible at this time." Mother turned the side of his mouth up as he shrugged, as if to say, *There's nothing either of us can do.*

Sharon felt like she'd been shot in the gut. "Not even for a day? I need to see him."

"The commandant told me we can't spare a pilot right now because we have to keep the squadrons supplied with aircraft. When the Luftwaffe stops attacking, then he can start handing out leaves." Mother held his hands out front as if they could cool her anger.

"Shit!"

Mother handed her a chit. "A Hurricane for Coltishall."

"Where the hell is that?" Sharon grabbed the chit and walked away. *Why are you so mad at him? It's not like he's handing out leaves.*

"Northeast of London. Close to Norwich," Mother said.

Sharon was still fuming when she collected the new Hurricane from the factory. Its two-hundred-mile-an-hour cruising speed made the trip to Norwich in thirty minutes.

She only smiled after the fighter settled gently onto the grass.

A mechanic waved at her as she taxied closer to the hangars. She guided the aircraft onto a concrete apron and shut it down.

Sharon stepped out onto the wing and pulled off her flying helmet.

"Oi!" the mechanic said. "Can't say I've ever seen a woman flying a Hurricane before."

Sharon glared at him.

A horizontal crease appeared between his black eyebrows and his black close-cropped hair. "Honestly, I meant nothin' by it."

Sharon stepped off the trailing edge of the wing. "Forget it. It's me. I'm in a foul mood."

"Don't see why you should be after a landing like that. Bloody smooth piece of work, that was." The mechanic went to the tail and began to lift and push.

*Don't take your foul mood out on him.* She ducked under the wing and pushed the leading edge as they guided the Hurricane back into the hangar.

"Thanks." The mechanic took a couple of deep breaths. "I'd offer to shake your hand, but mine are. . ." He displayed his oil-stained hands to her and began to wipe them with a rag he pulled out of the back pocket of his coveralls.

Sharon heard the sound of uneven footfalls and creaking leather.

"Where the hell is the other Hurricane? I told Group I needed two!"

The mechanic blanched.

Sharon turned to face a squadron leader who stumped across the floor by swinging his legs around in a close approximation of walking. He stopped and stood there, his feet apart and his fists on his hips. "Well? Where the hell is the other one?"

"Just the one so far, sir." The mechanic stood at attention.

The Squadron leader looked at Sharon. "Who the hell are you, somebody's girlfriend?"

"The pilot." Sharon felt her face turning red, and smiled when she sensed a fight brewing.

"What's your name?"

*Enough of this.* "Who the hell are you?"

The squadron leader turned his head to one side as though looking down a gun sight and glared at her. "Douglas Bader!"

"Sharon Lacey!" Sharon glared right back.

"Well, where is the other Hurricane?" Bader asked.

"How the hell would I know?" Sharon took a step forward and crossed her arms.

Bader threw his head back and laughed. The bellow filled the inside of the hangar.

The mechanic chuckled. To Sharon's ears, it sounded like nervous relief.

"You the same Sharon Lacey who shot down five in one day?" Bader asked.

*Shit, everyone at an airfield seems to have heard about it.* "That's right."

"Bloody marvelous! News travels fast around the squadrons when it comes to pilots and their scores. Your story in particular has lots of people wagging their tongues. The best I've ever done is two in one day. Join me for a cup of tea."

"Make it coffee," Sharon said.

"Have it your way! Come along, then." Bader swung around and began clumping his way out of the hangar.

Sharon had to hurry to keep up.

"I saw you land. You've got the touch. Where are you from?" Bader asked.

"Canada."

"Where in Canada?" He huffed as he hurried along.

"Calgary."

Bader stopped and turned. "Same town Willie McKnight is from! He's a hell of a pilot, too!" He started up again and led the way to the canteen. As he walked through the open tent flap, he said, "A cup of coffee for Sharon here and tea for me."

Within minutes, a group of pilots had gathered around Bader's table, and he was introducing Sharon. "Go on, tell them about how you downed five in one day," Bader said.

Sharon looked at the coffee in her cup. *How the hell did I get myself into this situation?* "I don't think anyone would be interested in that."

Stan, another Canadian, said, "You thought wrong."

So she told them the story.

Eric said, "You just lined them up and let the bullets fall into their cockpits?"

"Yes." Sharon looked around the table, trying to gauge their reactions.

Bader shrugged. "Bloody hell."

"Bloody good shooting," Stan said.

"How come your face isn't in all of the papers like Douglas over here?" Eric asked.

"I don't want. . ." *Let me get a word in!*

"Well?" Stan faced Bader.

Bader stood up, put his right foot on a chair, and pulled up his pant leg to reveal an artificial limb. "If you had two tin legs, then the newspapers would want to talk with you, too!"

Sharon found herself joining in on the laughter.

# CHAPTER 24
## [ SATURDAY, AUGUST 31, 1940 ]

**Mother stood outside of the door to the dispersal hut.** The evening light was pink. It accented his grey hair.

Sharon sat down and loosened her tie. *Six deliveries in one day. I'm beat.*

Mother said, "RAF losses have been heavy today. I need a pilot with night flying experience to make a delivery. Two squadrons are in desperate need of replacement aircraft before tomorrow morning."

"Do I have to wear a bloody tie?" Sharon asked.

Mother smiled. "Leave the tie. The Anson is waiting to take you to Castle Bromwich."

"Where am I going after that?"

"Tangmere. You'll have an overnight stay and be picked up first thing in the morning."

The sun was down when she took off from Castle Bromwich in a brand-spanking-new Spitfire. On takeoff, she caught the familiar scent of shit rising from the sewage pond at the end of the runway.

Within minutes, she reached two thousand feet, trimmed the aircraft, and headed south for the coast.

It was a clear night, and the stars seemed brighter due to the blackout.

She checked her watch, estimating her time to Tangmere, then looked out again. She recalled a summer night swim in a lake north of her home in Canada. The fear that something was lurking in the depths, stalking her from the shadows. *This isn't much like the nights of flying back home. Keep your head on a swivel, clear your tail with a quick turn to the right or left, then get back on course.*

She knew she was west of London, but could not see it until the searchlights sent ever-widening cones of light into the darkness. The anti-aircraft guns opened up, sending blazing rounds into the sky on her left.

*It looks beautiful.* Then she remembered the people on the ground being bombed, and the bombers in the shadows desperately trying to avoid detection.

She looked to her left for any signs of other aircraft, especially the telltale glow of exhaust. Nothing.

Behind her, nothing.

Just in case, she did a quick 360-degree turn, stick back into her belly, keeping the nose up with rudder. She felt herself being pushed down into the seat. Nothing on her tail.

She knew she was close to Tangmere when she saw the luminescent glow of ocean waves rolling up against the shore. Then she could smell the sea.

Sharon looked right and left, saw the runway lights, and lined up for her circuit.

A green Very light flared into the sky to signal she was clear to land.

After she landed, she taxied to the light of an open hangar door where, after shutdown, the new aircraft was pushed inside, and the big doors closed to hide their location.

Five men swarmed over the aircraft to ready it for tomorrow's expected battle as she stepped off the wing.

No one said a word to her or even seemed to notice as she pulled off her flight helmet and combed out her hair with her fingers.

She walked out the hangar's side door, closed it behind her, and was enveloped in darkness. She put one foot carefully in front of the other, listening for muffled conversation that would lead her to the dispersal hut.

# CHAPTER 25
## [ SUNDAY, SEPTEMBER 1, 1940 ]

**Douglas, the ATA pilot with the stocky physique,** flew the Anson with an athlete's grace. Sharon dozed, leaning against the window after her last delivery of the day.

They landed at White Waltham after sunset.

Sharon woke to a hand on her shoulder.

"Time to wake up. We're home." Douglas stepped back and waited for her to unbuckle and get up. He squeezed himself through the opening after Sharon was out the back door.

The dispersal hut was empty, so she stowed her gear and began the walk home.

*It's funny how you get used to the blackout.* She looked ahead into the night and waited for her eyes to adapt. The blackout was complete. *Yet I know where I am by the feel of the road.*

*There — I can see the dividing line between the trees and the sky. Not far now.* She quickened her pace.

She smelled smoke.

When she reached the front door of the cottage, the stink was stronger. She put the key in the lock, turned it carefully, and eased the door open. Cool air breezed past her.

"It's okay — it's just smoke." Linda's voice came from the kitchen.

Sharon closed the door behind her. The air above their heads was white with smoke. She looked to see if the letters were still on the ottoman.

"But I wanted to surprise her," Sean said.

Sharon stepped into the kitchen.

Linda and Sean had their backs to her and were looking at something smoldering in the sink.

The kitchen window was open.

"What will Sharon say?" Sean asked.

"We won't tell her," Linda said.

"It'll be our secret. This is a nice surprise. Sorry I'm so late," Sharon said.

Sean turned. Surprise and delight made his eyes seem brighter.

She almost fell over when he lunged and wrapped his arms around her. His head caught her under the chin. She closed her eyes, saw stars, and tried to maintain her balance. "Boy, it's good to see the two of you. Let me sit down."

Sean sat down next to her. "Linda had to see the doctor, so we came down on the train."

Linda sat across from them. She was wearing loose-fitting tan slacks and a white blouse. There were worry lines across her forehead. "We had a wonderful supper planned, but you know what a disaster I am in the kitchen."

Sharon put her arm around Sean's shoulders. "How's Honeysuckle?"

"Worried about Michael," Sean said.

Sharon sent a puzzled look in Linda's direction.

"We haven't heard from him since he left the farm with you. We're worried because we know the kind of work he does."

"What kind of work does he do? I mean, he says so little about what he really does," Sharon said.

Linda nodded. "It's the fact that he's so damned secretive about so much of what he does, but will talk at length about some of the bigger problems of the war. I think he might be in France again."

"How would he get there?" Sharon asked.

"We were hoping you would know. Honeysuckle said you met with Michael at some kind of secret air base that everyone else thinks is a farm," Linda said.

"Gibraltar Farm. It's all very hush-hush. I've delivered a few Lysanders there."

The words fell out of Linda's mouth in a jumble. "He would need a way to get into France without attracting notice. He knows the language. He has contacts in the country — people he went to school with. The Lysander can land almost anywhere."

"We know that people are getting in and out of France in Lysanders," Sharon said. "They were talking about putting long-range tanks into one I delivered. And when I was at Tangmere last night, a Lysander landed, refueled, and took off. It headed out over the Channel. It returned just after sunrise when the Anson came to pick me up. They kept the Lysander at the far end of the field. It was like that night when I first met Michael, and you had that fight with him. So we know part of the picture, but there's still too much we don't know." Sharon felt Sean's head leaning against her shoulder. "Maybe we'd best move to the sitting room."

Fifteen minutes later, Linda said, "He's asleep. He was so excited about coming to see you, he didn't sleep last night or on the train. I'll get a blanket." She stood up from the couch and went to the closet. She pulled out a blanket as Sharon eased away from her brother and placed a pillow under his head.

Linda covered him with the blanket. "He and Mom are getting along very well. He's made her young again."

"How's he handling what happened to his parents?" Sharon looked at him sleeping there and wondered at the cherubic serenity of a sleeping child.

Linda looked at her friend. "Let's have a cup of tea. I think I can manage that without causing smoke." She went into the kitchen and turned off the light in the sitting room.

Sharon sat down at the kitchen table. "I don't need a cup of tea for bad news."

Linda filled the kettle and set it on the stove. "He has nightmares."

Sharon shook her head. "I can't get away. All leaves have been cancelled."

"No one is blaming you. And speaking of nightmares, you look like you haven't slept in quite some time." Linda sat down across from her friend.

"I have no problem falling asleep. It's just that I usually wake up after being shot down in flames with my fists pounding against the inside of the canopy. Even after I wake up, I can still smell burning flesh and hair." Sharon leaned up against the kitchen wall.

"I have a similar recurring nightmare. It's even more vivid after I've had a glass of beer." Linda smiled.

"Well, I'll have to try a pint before bed, then." Sharon said sarcastically.

"I wouldn't recommend it." Linda got up to pour the boiling water into a teapot. "Mother's really worried about Michael this time. She said that last time she didn't hear from him, but didn't worry as much. She thinks something has happened to him. In case you hadn't noticed, Honeysuckle believes in intuition." She put the lid on the teapot, then brought the pot and cups to the table. "And Marmaduke has been dropping by unexpectedly. That's been pretty unsettling for her."

Sharon sat up straight. "What's he done to her?"

"Asking questions. Mostly about you and Sean. Mother is getting tired of him sniffing around." Linda poured their tea. The sweet, sharp scent of it filled the kitchen.

"You know that I hired a lawyer, Walter McGregor, after Marmaduke tried to get me to sign away all rights to my mother's inheritance." Sharon blew steam off the top of the tea before she sipped.

"You've got him worried, and he thinks Honeysuckle might know something about it." Linda looked in the front room to check if Sean had woken.

"That's probably what's happened. I'm afraid I've brought no end of trouble to you and your family."

Linda looked at her friend. "How extraordinary that you would see the situation from that point of view! We don't see it that way at all."

"How do you see it?"

"My mother thinks she's had a second chance with her childhood friend. She says that Leslie was a sister to her. I've gained a friend as well. Michael, he's. . . I've never seen him like this. He's usually so self-contained and self-assured."

Sharon went to open her mouth, then closed it. *What can I say in response to that?*

Linda's mouth formed a straight line. "I'd better be off to bed. Sean and I need to catch the early train to make it to Grinstead."

"What's the matter?"

"Michael's my brother. I just don't want to see him hurt."

"And you think I'll hurt him?"

Linda turned. "Not intentionally."

"This is all new to me, Linda." Sharon leaned forward.

"I know. I'm just worried about him. He's the only brother I have."

Sharon decided to change the subject. "Do you need another skin graft operation?"

Linda did not turn as she went up the stairs. "That's what I'll find out tomorrow."

# CHAPTER 26
## [ MONDAY, SEPTEMBER 2, 1940 ]

**Sharon woke with her nose bent up against** the floral pattern of the wing-backed chair. She heard Sean snoring. She sat up and looked at her wristwatch. "Shit!"

She kissed Sean on the forehead, tucked the blanket more tightly around him, grabbed her kit, and stepped out the door.

By the time she returned that evening, her uniform carried the telltale signs of having spent at least part of the day in a slit trench.

Linda opened the door. She was wearing a white blouse and baggy black trousers. Linda looked at her friend. "What happened to you?"

"I delivered a Spitfire to Kenley. I'm surprised you didn't hear all the noise. The Luftwaffe arrived, and I headed for cover." Sharon looked around her friend. "Where's Sean?"

"In the loo. Come on. Get cleaned up. We're going out for fish and chips. No more suffering through my disasters in the kitchen." Linda stood back from the door.

Sharon stepped past her. "Sean! Hurry up and let me in the bath. I need to get cleaned up."

Linda closed the front door.

Sharon turned. "What did the doctors say?"

Linda smiled. "They say I'm healing well, and I need to come back in three weeks to see about another skin graft."

Footsteps pounded on the floorboards. Sean appeared in the hallway. "Where are we going?"

"Out for supper. There's a wonderful place just down the road." Linda looked at Sharon. "We'll eat after your sister gets cleaned up."

In half an hour, Sharon was back downstairs, wearing a clean pair of trousers and a blue blouse.

"Let's go!" Linda limped her way out the door and down the road to the pub.

Sean ran ahead, then ran back until he could smell the food. He met them at the front door of the pub.

They ate outside, using their fingers to eat the chips and fish.

Linda licked her fingers. "God, I've missed this."

"I'm sorry about Michael and me. I don't know what to say when I'm around him. He's always so nice to me, and he's your brother. The problem is, when I'm around him, I can't think clearly." Sharon stuffed a chip in her mouth. *Just shut up. Things were going so well. Why did you have to bring that up? Now Linda will be upset.*

Linda turned to her friend. "What did you say?"

"About what?" Half a chip fell out of Sharon's mouth.

Linda and Sean began to laugh.

"This is the first time in a long time I've felt like maybe I'm. . ." Sharon said.

"Normal?" Linda asked.

"Full?" Sean asked.

"At peace. Just right now, at this moment, I feel at peace. I think that's what I'm trying to say."

# CHAPTER 27
## [ THURSDAY, SEPTEMBER 5, 1940 ]

**Sharon lingered over a cup of coffee** as she watched the air-craftsmen tucking in one of White Waltham's Ansons for the night. *Not much point in getting in a rush to go home since Linda and Sean left. And, if I'm being honest with myself, I'm not ready to read another of my mother's letters.*

"Lacey!" Sharon looked up.

One of the pilots waved at her. "Mother is looking for you!"

Sharon stood up and walked to the dispersal hut.

"There you are!" Mother waved her over. He had a chit in his hand. His hair hung over his ears and back collar. He never seemed to have a day off and, as a result, didn't have time to get his hair cut.

*I thought I was done for the day.*

"Someone's got their wind up! You ever hear of Gibraltar Farm?" Mother asked.

Sharon nodded. *I wonder if Michael will be there.*

"They've got an urgent order for a replacement Lysander, and they specifically asked for you. I wrote the directions down." He pointed at the back of the chit.

Sharon took the paper and read the back. It told her where to pick up the Lysander. This time, it was just on the southwest side of London. "It's very close."

"A car is on its way to pick you up. You'll receive more directions when you reach the assembly hangar." Mother pointed at Sharon's coffee cup. "Have another one of those."

The driver of the black Austin arrived twenty minutes later. He never got out of the car, never said a word to her after asking, "Are you Sharon Lacey?" and never stopped until they reached the small airfield where the new Lysander sat outside of the open doors of the hangar. The sun was just at the horizon. It painted the surrounding trees in a variety of vibrant shades of green. Blackbirds skimmed the grass, then climbed for the higher branches of the trees.

A mechanic sat and watched her from a chair set just inside the hangar door. He sipped from a cup as she carried her parachute, helmet, and bag over to the Lysander.

"I was told you would have some instructions for me." She turned to watch the Austin sedately fart away in a cloud of blue exhaust.

The mechanic reached into the breast pocket of his coveralls and handed her an envelope. He put his tea down and walked over to the Lysander, where he leaned his shoulder up against the fuselage before crossing his arms and legs.

*This is bloody ridiculous. Closed-mouthed men hanging about, and nobody tells me a bloody thing!* Sharon tore open the envelope and read the instructions: "Tangmere — land on the green Very light signal, and near its point of origin. Then taxi to the waiting petrol bowser."

She was airborne ten minutes later as dusk turned to night.

In less than thirty minutes, a green Very light flare snaked its way up into the sky at Tangmere airfield. As instructed, she landed close to the flare's point of origin.

A torch waved its beam from side to side. It directed her to the petrol bowser parked next to a car.

Sharon shut down, undid her harness, and climbed down the side of the aircraft.

The driver of the truck pulled the fuel hose over to the Lysander. The nozzle clanked against the neck of the fuel tank. The scent of petrol filled the air as he began to top up the tanks.

Someone touched Sharon's elbow. She turned and saw the silhouette of a man who said, "Miss Lacey? Please come over to the car."

She followed him. *His voice is familiar.* She saw a white triangle of cloth reaching from his shoulder to his belly. "What happened to your arm?"

"Hit a bomb crater when I landed this morning. Made a bloody mess of my kite and my shoulder." He brought out a torch and shone it on the hood of the car. "There's a map in the back seat. Bring it out, please."

*Now I remember who it is.* "How are you otherwise, Richard?" Sharon opened the back door of the car. The inside smelled of liniment and mint. She felt around and retrieved the map.

"You have a very good memory. Open the map up, would you?" There was a no-nonsense tone to Richard's voice.

Sharon got a glimpse of his scarred face from the glare of the flashlight. When she saw the map, her nerves got the best of her and her back twitched. "It's a map of France!"

"Of course it is." He pointed at the south. "And this is Morlaix. About one hundred and fifty miles southwest of here."

Sharon could feel his eyes on her, as if waiting for her to say what was on her mind. "You're telling me I'm flying to France?"

"Um." Richard hesitated. "Actually, I'm asking you to consider flying to Morlaix, dropping off some cargo, and then returning with an agent."

"When?" Sharon asked.

"Tonight. I was supposed to make the pickup, but the plan has to change. You see, with the Battle of Britain going on, and the shortage of experienced pilots, there really is no one else available, as far as I can see."

*I'll take that as a compliment.* "Who is this agent?"

"I believe you met him the night we met. He's the brother of that friend of yours who knows how to defend herself. If memory serves correctly, so do you." Richard kept his finger on the map. The lens of the torch remained focused there.

*Michael!* "Is he all right?"

"Frankly, we're not sure. We received a report that the he was betrayed and the Nazis are hunting him down."

"Have you calculated the compass heading?" Sharon felt a combination of excitement and dread.

"Yes." He tapped the map with his forefinger. "You just follow this heading, then turn left down the Rivière de Morlaix until you find the viaduct. It's like one series of arches built on top of another. Then you travel fourteen miles south of the arches. The landing site is there. There will be nine torches in a line — make sure it's exactly nine — to indicate the field. You land and aim the Lizzie into wind. They will do the offloading and loading. You keep the engine running, and be ready to take off at a moment's notice. Use full flap for a short field takeoff."

"What about using the landing light?"

"That's up to you. Just be very careful. The last time I was in the area, I think I saw a Messerschmitt 110 nosing about."

Sharon looked at the map, memorizing the shoreline and compass headings. "What altitude do you fly?"

"I like to keep it at or below five hundred feet over the Channel. I'm not sure if the Germans have radar on the coast yet, but I don't want to take the chance. Just make sure your altimeter is set properly, or you'll end up in the drink." Richard shut off the torch.

"Anything else?" Sharon folded the map, tucked it in the pocket of her flight suit, and took the torch. "I might need this."

"Be sure you're back before dawn. After sunrise, you'll be a sitting duck for any Luftwaffe morning patrols over the Channel."

Sharon nodded. She turned toward the Lysander. The man doing the refueling wound the hose back into the petrol bowser.

Richard walked over the rear cockpit and reached for the ladder.

"What are you doing?"

"I'm coming along to show you the way."

"No, you're not. If I don't make it back, you're going to tell Michael's family and my brother, Sean, what happened." She stood on one leg of the undercarriage.

"How do I get in touch with them?" Richard asked.

"Ask around Gibraltar Farm. You'll figure it out. They live near Ilkley. The family name is Townsend."

Richard tapped the side of his head with a finger. "Got it. Townsend from Ilkley. Now, you make sure you use up the fuel in the auxiliary tank first. That way she flies better on the way home. That's when you'll have extra weight in the rear seat."

In fifteen minutes, Sharon was over the Channel and on course. The darkness wasn't total, but it was close. She looked at the stars on her right side. She thought back to night flights over the Canadian prairies. The voice of her mother's boss came to her. *You can find your way home by using the stars. Just pick your star or constellation. I like the Big and Little Dippers. Remember where the stars are located on the windscreen when you fly outbound and keep them there; I like to leave a thumbprint on the canopy as a guide. Keep the stars in the same place on the other side of the canopy on the return flight. That way, you keep your eyes on the sky where they should be, and not always on your instruments.*

Sharon cycled her eyes from the instruments to the stars and to the darkness, ever watchful for a subtle wavering shadow or the glow of exhaust indicating another aircraft.

She checked her watch and looked down to her left. The island of Guernsey was a darker shade against the ocean. The luminescence of the waves against its shoreline framed the near side of the island. *I wish I'd taken the time to stop at the bathroom.*

She made a mental calculation of the time it would take to make the next landfall and checked it against Richard's numbers. She estimated thirty minutes, if she flew directly to Morlaix, which would make her on time for the rendezvous.

*Don't think about Michael. Don't think about what to say. Keep your eyes open, and keep your mind on the job. There will be time for talk after you land back at Tempsford. It's eighty miles to the viaduct, then turn south.*

She made landfall twenty minutes later, and eight minutes after that, she spotted the double arches of the Viaduc de Morlaix. The viaduct's distinctive outline passed beneath her as she cruised at five hundred feet and headed south.

She estimated five minutes to the rendezvous and was thirty seconds off.

A series of faint flashes made her turn right. She counted the light from the torches.

*Eight? No, there are nine.* She throttled back, set the flaps, and began her circuit.

Her eyes scanned the sky, looking for any evidence of other aircraft — any telltale blue or yellow from an engine exhaust. "Nothing."

She turned onto her final approach, checked her airspeed, and dropped over a stand of trees. The wheels skipped onto the pasture, with its line of torches marking the makeshift runway.

Sharon backed off on the throttle, then applied the brakes.

The Lysander was almost at a full stop. She opened the throttle, pushed the rudder, and swung the tail around to be ready for takeoff.

Out of the dark, silhouettes appeared. They opened the hatch below and to her right. She felt the aircraft shiver. A pair of men ran back into the shadows carrying a box.

She watched as a man was hoisted up the side of the fuselage. He slid the rear canopy open.

Sharon felt the night air at the back of her neck. She heard the rear canopy slide shut. Someone pounded on the side of the fuselage.

To her right, she saw a man on the ground. The torch illuminated his face. He smiled and held a thumb up in front of his face before backing away.

Sharon opened the throttle. When enough speed built up, she pushed the stick forward and eased the Lysander off of the field and over the trees.

She leveled off at five hundred feet and set a direct course for Tempsford. The viaduct was on her right now. Sharon checked the stars, found the constellation she'd been navigating by, and set it inside a windshield frame on her left side.

*Now take a look.* She twisted around to see over her right shoulder. Through the narrow space between the auxiliary tank and the windscreen, she could see a pair of smiling eyes watching her. Outside of the cockpit, she caught a glimpse of something far more sinister.

Lines of tracer bullets streamed toward them.

Sharon instinctively shoved the stick hard over to the left.

A pair of cannon shells smashed through the right side of the cockpit.

She turned tighter to the left. She felt herself being dragged back down in the seat.

The attacking aircraft flew overtop of them on the right side. There was a glimpse of blue-yellow exhaust, twin engines, and twin tails.

"Messerschmitt 110!" she said.

It climbed, coming around for a second attack run.

Pain radiated from Sharon's right thigh, just above her knee. She leveled out. *You know what needs to be done. He's faster than you, but he also thinks you're easy prey. His blood is running hot. He wants this kill. Use it against him.* Sharon eased the throttle back and lowered some flap.

She looked at the airspeed indicator. Its glass cover was shattered, and the instrument's arrows pointed uselessly toward her feet. *Fly by feel.*

Sharon looked over her shoulder as the 110 turned and climbed. A predator rising into the black. Its passage marked by stars, which blinked off, then on.

*Let him think he has you dead to rights.* She burned with the primal, protective instinct mothers feel when one of theirs is threatened. "You come after Michael and me, and I'm gonna kill you bastards!"

Sharon put her hand on the throttle.

The Messerschmitt leveled off, turned toward her and closed to within one hundred yards.

Sharon added throttle, pushed the stick hard over to the right, and watched the 110 try to follow.

He fired wildly. The tracers burned a falling arc through the sky she'd left a moment ago.

The Lysander's right wing pointed at the ground. She estimated her height as she swung the stick hard over to the left, always keeping in mind that she must get them closer to the Channel.

She looked up and to her left. The 110 climbed, stall-turned, reversed direction, and dove on her. Sharon rolled the Lysander on its back, pulled back on the stick, and eased off the throttle.

Darkness filled her sightline. She pulled out of the inverted vertical dive with the wind shrieking through the holes in the cockpit, then
leveled out at what she estimated to be one hundred feet above the
ground and added throttle. *They're too heavy to follow that manoeuvre
when they're this close to the ground. You've just killed two more men.*

She looked over her right shoulder as she turned.

She caught the silhouette of the 110 pulling out of his dive.

Sharon watched as the Messerschmitt appeared to level out at the
bottom of a split S turn.

The belly of the Nazi fighter was illuminated by a splash of sparks
when it touched the ground. Then the Messerschmitt and its crew
were transformed into heat and light.

Sharon closed her eyes too late. The fireball blinded her. Her night
vision was gone for the time being.

She looked down at her compass. It had been shattered by the
same hot metal that had struck her leg. The wind blew through the
holes in the fuselage and made her eyes tear. She pulled her goggles
down over her eyes.

Sharon climbed to what she hoped was five hundred feet and headed
in the direction of what she thought was the northeast. *Give it a few
minutes. Your night vision will return. You've got time now.*

She looked out the left window. Her constellation was there. She
lined it up in the spot she'd chosen on the windscreen. *That'll get us
home.* She trimmed the Lysander for level flight.

Sharon looked down. She saw the jagged effervescence of the
French coastline and made a mental calculation of how far it was to
the Isle of Guernsey.

She felt a touch on her shoulder. Sharon turned to see Michael's
hand. The silhouette of his face was visible. She imagined him smiling encouragement.

She caught a whiff of gasoline fumes from the auxiliary fuel tank
behind her seat. *There must be a hole in it. Thank you, Richard, for
telling me to drain it first.* She checked the instruments, which still func-
tioned. Engine temperature and oil pressure were where they should be.

*Do something about your leg.* Sharon reached for the map with her right hand, held it over the wound on her thigh, and pressed it tight. The pain made her jerk back in her seat. Her hand lifted. The wind blew the map back over her shoulder. *Hold your hand right there on your leg! You can't pass out now! You have no idea how much blood you've lost.* She looked at her watch. *Another twenty minutes to Guernsey, and at least that long to Tempsford. An hour. Hang on for an hour.*

Sharon wiggled the toes in her right flight boot. *My foot feels wet. The blood must be running down my leg.*

Michael kept his hand on her shoulder.

Sharon breathed deeply. *Calm. You've got to keep calm.* She kept one hand on the leg wound. The other worked the controls.

They passed Guernsey. She cocked her head to the right. Michael gave her another squeeze on the shoulder.

Sharon began to shiver. *Another half an hour. Plan ahead for the landing. Hold onto the wound.*

She flew the last thirty minutes with her teeth gritted while going through the landing preparations in her mind. Holding pressure on the wound. Holding on to the control stick with her left hand, even though her arm and hand were shaking with fatigue. Holding on because she needed to pee so badly, she could almost taste it.

Half an hour later, Sharon saw blue where the horizon met the sky.

By the time they reached the coast, she could make out a few landmarks, like the Isle of Wight.

Tempsford was just a few miles inland. She looked down at her leg and saw a bloody stain on the coveralls under her hand.

She lifted her right hand from the wound, wiped it across her chest, and used it to hold the controls while giving her left a rest. She began her landing checklist.

Sharon spotted the airfield and began her approach. On finals, the green Very light streaked into the sky. She landed, using the rudder pedals to guide them toward the straight lines and right angles of the white control tower, a decidedly ugly structure.

After stopping in front of the tower, she idled the engine until the temperature dropped, shut it down, and switched off.

She looked to her left and right. *No one's about.* She heard the canopy slide open behind her. She looked at the shattered remains of the aircraft's instruments. There were holes in the windshield and others she hadn't noticed in the skin of the fuselage.

A bloody face appeared on the other side of the hole in the windscreen.

"Who the hell are you?"

"It's me. Michael." There was blood caked along his hairline and in his eyebrows. His cheeks were streaked with it. His shirt was stained with it.

"What happened to you?"

"Let's get you out of there first and worry about explanations afterward." He opened the canopy and helped her release her harness. In his haste to get her out, his hand brushed against her breast.

"Oi, I hardly know you." Sharon began to giggle. "After a little slap and tickle, are we?"

"You must be going into shock. Come on! Stand up. I'll help you get down." Michael steadied her with his hands. He guided her right foot outside the cockpit and down to where the wing strut and undercarriage met. When she went to step on the concrete apron, her right leg shook. He grabbed her under the armpits and set her on the ground.

*My knees feel a little weak.* She looked down at her thigh and the bloody stain there.

"Let's get you to the infirmary," Michael said.

Sharon stood up and shrugged him off. She limped toward the tower. "First things first. I need to pee."

o *Sharon winced when the doctor tugged the syringe* out of her thigh.

"Give that a minute or two, then we'll stitch you up." The doctor wore a white lab coat. He had very few hairs on his head, except those growing out of his nose, ears, and eyebrows.

"Were you in the last war, Doctor?" Michael stood near the door with his arms crossed over the front of a jacket stained with his blood.

A redheaded nurse of about twenty-five handed him a square of white gauze. "Hold this on the wound, and I'll get you cleaned up."

The doctor said, "I spent three years in the Great War."

Sharon looked at the doctor's weary eyes. *I think I'd prefer it if the nurse stitched me up.*

"Don't worry, young man. I'll take good care of your girlfriend," the doctor said.

Michael blushed.

*I kinda like the sound of that*, Sharon thought.

The doctor washed his hands, dried them, then picked out a suture. "Ladies first." He began to work on stitching Sharon's thigh.

The nurse asked, "How did you get the nick on the head?"

Michael said, "Sharon was avoiding a Messerschmitt. It attacked, and she turned us upside down. I was holding on for dear life, but not well enough to stop my head from banging against the frame of the cockpit."

"What happened to the Messerschmitt?" The nurse held Michael's hand against the wound on his forehead with one hand and efficiently wiped the blood away from his face with the other.

*Hey, get your hands off of him!* Sharon thought.

Michael looked at Sharon. "She flew him right into the ground. He blew up."

Sharon felt a tug at her thigh. The lips of the wound were coming together.

"Should only take ten or eleven stitches," the doctor said. "In case you're wondering."

"That's all?" Sharon asked.

"I could do more, if you like. It looks like a piece of shrapnel ripped open your leg and the flight suit." The doctor smiled. "The cut is long, but not too deep, fortunately."

"No, it just seemed. . ." Sharon said.

"When you can't see how badly you're hurt, your mind can play tricks. By the looks of your clothes, you've been soaked in sweat." The doctor straightened up. "You're done. Now it's time to repair your boyfriend."

Sharon looked at Michael. "You need to phone Honeysuckle."

Michael frowned.

"Who's Honeysuckle?" the nurse asked.

"My mother," Michael said.

"She's been very worried," Sharon said.

"By all means, you must phone," the doctor said. "There's one in the room just down the hallway."

Michael shook his head.

"What the hell are we playing at, then?" Sharon asked.

"What do you mean?" Michael asked.

"Perhaps we should leave and let you two sort things out," the nurse said.

"Do what you like!" Sharon kept her focus on Michael. "Are we together or are we not?"

"We haven't really discussed that," Michael said.

"We are discussing it now. So what is it? Are we or aren't we?" Sharon swung her feet onto the floor.

"We are. It's just that there are other people's lives at stake. There are rules I'm supposed to follow. People who I need to report to."

"If I followed the rules, we wouldn't be here having this conversation. You'd still be in France."

"You don't know what I know about the war. You don't know what information I have to pass on to my superiors."

"Of course I don't, but you can still make a phone call to your mother to let her know you're safe."

Michael looked exasperated. "Yes."

Sharon limped to the door. "I'll make the call while you get stitched up."

As she walked into the hallway, she heard the doctor say, "She's a bit of a handful."

Michael said, "She's that, all right."

"I hope you're not going to let her get away from you," the doctor said.

"No. Definitely not."

"Good man," the doctor said.

Sharon smiled as she made her way down the hallway to the phone.

She sat down in the chair behind the desk and began to dial. Her hand was shaking. It took three tries. Finally, the phone was ringing at the other end.

"Hello?"

"Honeysuckle? It's me, Sharon." Fatigue was a cup of warm milk filling her up.

"Are you all right?"

"I'm fine. Michael is here. He's fine as well." Sharon closed her eyes.

"You sound tired," Honeysuckle said.

"I am. I just wanted you to know that we're okay." Sharon hung up.

After Michael was tended to, he found her there, snoring with her head cradled on her elbow, dead to the world.

# CHAPTER 28
## [ JANUARY 1941 ]

**"I've noticed that other people will talk** about the fact that you're an ace. Yet I've never heard you mention it." Mother sat across from Sharon inside the White Waltham dispersal hut.

Sharon shrugged. She wore her fleece-lined Irvine jacket with a pair of coveralls underneath and still couldn't stay warm in the damp British cold. *Give me a cold, sunny January day on the prairies anytime.*

"It was the same after the last war. Most often, the ones who were in the thick of it didn't want to talk about it. While the ones who never got near the front line talked like they'd fought and won the war single-handedly." Mother picked up a chit and waved it at Sharon. "This delivery is a bit unusual."

"How's that?" Sharon reached for the paper.

"You're to report to Salisbury Hall."

"Where's that?" Sharon took the chit.

"Northwest of London. If memory serves, Salisbury Hall has an actual moat." Mother winked.

"You're joking!"

"Not a bit of it. By the way, how's Sean?"

"Fine. I get a letter almost every day. It sounds like he's fitting in. I miss him, of course." Sharon felt the tears brimming.

"That brings up another matter. You've been granted a week's leave, starting the day after tomorrow."

"Thank you, Mother!" Sharon stood up, reached across the table, and hugged him.

"Let me finish." Mother's ears were red from blushing.

Sharon released him.

"We'll set up a delivery for you somewhere near Ilkley. You deserve a leave after the battle and all of the replacements you've delivered since then. You've been going non-stop. And we know, as do many of the pilots, that you did more than most."

Sharon frowned. *Linda gave more than I did.*

"I know, you'd rather it be kept quiet. Still, there are many of us at the flying end of things who know what you did. And, just between me, you, and the wall over there, that order for you to go to Salisbury Hall comes from the top."

Sharon cocked her head to one side. "You mean d'Erlanger?"

Mother nodded. "You always were a quick study. Can I conclude that d'Erlanger knows what you did?"

*He does indeed.* "Can I fetch you a cup of coffee?"

"Ah, an abrupt change in topic. I'll take that as a yes, then?" Mother put his forefinger to the bridge of his nose and winked at her.

"No flies on you." Sharon smiled. "Do you want a bloody cup of coffee or not?"

"No, thank you. Better be on your way." He pointed in the general direction of the airfield. "Douglas just finished his walk around on the Anson."

"By the way, what happened to Roger?" Sharon asked.

Mother's eyes narrowed. "Drank himself into another kind of work."

Sharon grabbed her gear, went out the door, and strolled to the Anson. The leather of her flying boots was wet with last night's rain and this morning's dissipating patches of fog.

Douglas was strapping himself into the pilot's seat of the Anson. She tossed her gear in the rear door and climbed in after.

"Good morning, Sharon. We're off to Salisbury Hall." Douglas adjusted a throttle and flipped a switch.

"Anyone else off to exotic locales this morning?" Sharon sat down and strapped herself in just aft of the wing spar.

"Just you. A quick hop for me, then off to Duxford." Douglas opened his side window. "Clear!"

One propeller began to rotate. The engine coughed, then caught, and the propeller disappeared into a blur.

Douglas started the other engine. He glanced over his shoulder. "All secure?"

Sharon checked her harness and looked back to make sure the rear door was closed and latched. She nodded at Douglas.

The flight to Salisbury Hall took less than half an hour. Sharon looked down as Douglas passed over a two-storey manor house that looked to be half as big again as Lacey Manor. She spotted a twin-engined aircraft. It had black spinners and black tarps covering most of a yellow paint scheme. *I've never seen an airplane quite like that before.*

After Douglas landed, dropped her off, and departed, Sharon dodged puddles as she made her way over to the hangar for a closer look at the yellow aircraft.

A soldier pulled his rifle off of his shoulder and held it across his body. "Stand and be recognized."

Sharon stopped. *Not this again.*

"It's quite all right!" Gerard d'Erlanger stepped out of the hangar, followed by a pilot in a black flight suit who was unfamiliar to Sharon. "She's with the ATA. She's expected. My fault. I should have given you advanced warning."

The soldier put his rifle back on his shoulder and turned his back on them.

"Sharon Lacey, this is Geoffrey," d'Erlanger said.

The other pilot, with the unruly hair and a ready smile, offered Sharon his hand. "A distinct pleasure, Miss Lacey."

She shook it. "Thank you." *That's the best I can come up with? Thank you?*

"I've suggested that Geoffrey here take you up for a flight in a new aircraft that is being tested and will soon be on the front lines. A word or two from Geoffrey in the right ear will go a long way to opening up all types of aircraft to ATA pilots such as yourself," d'Erlanger said.

"Gerard tells me you've done quite a variety of flying during the recent battles, and that you've had some rather unique experiences." Geoffrey smiled.

*What is he smiling about?*

"You do understand that what we are about to do is covered by the Official Secrets Act." Geoffrey stopped smiling to accentuate the sobriety of his announcement. "It's important that we keep knowledge of this aircraft secret before it reaches active service."

Sharon nodded. *What have I gotten myself into now?*

"All right, then, first things first. Follow along as I take you through the preflight check." Geoffrey walked toward the aircraft.

D'Erlanger walked in the direction of a nearby building, leaving Sharon next to a puddle of water. She followed Geoffrey, who stood under the nose of the aircraft and looked up through an access door. He propped a ladder up against the inside of the hatch. "We'll begin at the nose."

*He's very methodical, very thorough*, Sharon thought as he walked her around and underneath the aircraft. "What's it called?"

Geoffrey walked to the narrow ladder under the nose and held it steady. "I think it will be called the Mosquito." He indicated with his right hand that she should climb aboard.

Sharon stepped on the bottom rung of the ladder, climbed, and squeezed through the narrow opening, then crawled onto the floor of the aircraft. She stood up under the generous canopy. The aircraft smelled of wood and fresh paint.

Geoffrey's head popped through the opening. "Sit in the pilot's seat, please."

"What?"

"You didn't think we brought you up here just to watch, did you?" Geoffrey elbowed his way up through the opening and sat down beside her in the observer's seat. "Get strapped in. I'll talk you through all of the bells and whistles, and we'll see if you're as good as Gerard says you are."

After he explained the Mosquito's personality and remarkably few foibles to her, the aircraft was towed out to the taxiway. She started up first the right engine, and then the left. He talked her through the preflight checks. The power of the paired Merlin engines launched them on takeoff. Sharon focused on her instruments as they climbed through the solid overcast, then above it, into a white glaring wonderland at twenty thousand feet. She yelled with pure exhilaration at the thrill of it, the absolute joy as she sat between those two powerful engines where the forward visibility was remarkable. When she checked the airspeed, her jaw dropped. *This thing is fast!* Their hour in the air was over in what felt like ten short minutes.

After the landing and shutdown, Sharon followed Geoffrey across to his office, where d'Erlanger was talking on the telephone.

D'Erlanger hung up. "Well? How was the flight?"

Geoffrey said, "There's no problem here. I think that you understated Miss Lacey's abilities as a pilot. High-performance aircraft are her forte."

D'Erlanger nodded.

There was a knock at the door. It opened, and a tray arrived with a teapot, cream, sugar, and three cups.

After the batman left, d'Erlanger poured the tea, sat, and curled his fingers around the china.

Sharon added cream and sugar, then sat down.

Geoffrey sat down to complete the triangle.

Sharon took a sip. *This isn't at all bad.*

"There are a number of new aircraft that are about to become available to the RAF and the Navy. As a result, we will need someone to fly them, oversee the manuals for other ATA pilots, and provide assistance where necessary. Are you interested?" d'Erlanger asked.

Sharon frowned. "Are you offering me a new job?"

"And a promotion, actually. Quite frankly, you've earned it," d'Erlanger said.

"When do I start?"

D'Erlanger smiled. "You have a week's leave coming up?"

"Yes."

"Your orders will be waiting for you when you return to White Waltham." D'Erlanger took another sip of tea. "The RAF is going to experience tremendous expansion, even more profound than what we've already gone through. We have new aircraft to deliver and we need people to train the pilots who will fly them. And" — he glanced at Geoffrey — "there are still those who believe that women are not up to the work. You will help prove the naysayers wrong."

She frowned. *I'm to be a poster girl for the ATA?*

Geoffrey said, "Before you begin to think you're some kind of propaganda tool, think again. We need pilots whom young women will look up to, and who will teach them the skills they require to stay alive."

o **Later that evening,** Sharon sat down for supper in the White Waltham mess. She stared at a plate of mutton and beans. Her stomach groaned. She looked up at the other tables. Two tables away sat a pair of women a few years older than her. A dark-haired woman talked behind her hand and lifted her chin in Sharon's direction. The blonde looked at Sharon, frowned, and turned away.

In a moment, all that had happened in the past months filled her mind with a collage of impressions complete with scents, sounds, and sights. Linda, so excited about flying a Spitfire, then crash-landing her burning aircraft; the stink of her burning flesh. The first encounter with her father, and his death. Bullets from her guns falling into the cockpits of enemy bombers that exploded when they hit the ground. The sight and scent of blood dripping from the chin of her Spitfire. The exhilaration that came with surviving combat. Touching Sean's hand for the first time, then leaving him with Honeysuckle. It was at that moment that her mind began to process what she saw, what she felt, what she heard, and what she knew in a slightly yet significantly different way.

*It'll be interesting leading people like this. After what I've been through, why be afraid of them?* She stood, took her plate, and sat across from the two women.

"I don't know your names. Perhaps we could introduce ourselves?" Sharon looked down at the mutton, the marbled fat and the grey flesh.

The pilots looked at one another.

Sharon could see the sheen of sweat on the blonde's forehead. "Which one of you knows my uncle, Marmaduke Lacey, and his family?"

"How did you know that?" the dark-haired woman asked.

"I've met my uncle. I know how he operates. Hopefully, you will never have that pleasure." Sharon got up, left her food, and walked outside, where she could watch the blackbirds chattering, swooping, and diving. She stayed there until the sun set, then went home and got dressed for her date.

# CHAPTER 29

**Sharon took a breather** after walking two miles along the A660 roadway heading northwest toward Ilkley. Sean, Linda, Honeysuckle, and — if no pressing emergency delayed him — Michael would be waiting at the Townsend Farm. *Maybe it wasn't such a good idea to surprise them.* About eight hundred feet above her, the blue-grey clouds promised rain. She hefted the twenty-pound duffel bag. Its rope was rubbing a groove in her right shoulder. She was glad the bag was all that would fit in the luggage compartment in the back of the Spitfire she'd delivered to Leeds.

A two-door Morris van purred along the road. She smiled and looked hopefully at the driver. The Morris passed Sharon. Its red taillights came on. It pulled to the side of the road. Sharon ran to catch up.

She opened the passenger door and leaned inside.

"You're going to get wet. Get in," the driver said. Forty-something, with grey frizzy hair under a worn tweed cap, a tweedy jacket and slacks, and a blue woolen scarf wrapped around the neck, the sex of the driver was indeterminate.

"Are you going to Ilkley?" Sharon got a whiff of milk and chicken feathers.

Rain began to splatter against the windshield. The driver nodded and turned on the wipers. "I suggest you get in before we both get a soaking."

Sharon squeezed inside, put her bag on her lap, and shut the door.

"I'm Sharon." She looked sideways at the driver, who ground the gears while shifting into second.

"I know. That's why I stopped. You're the image of your mother. For a minute, I thought it was Leslie. Same brown hair. Same face." The driver double-clutched and shifted into third gear.

The rain intensified the stink of milk and chicken feathers. Sharon looked for a window crank.

"The window's broken. Don't worry, you'll get used to the smell in a minute or two. I do my egg, cream, and chicken deliveries every other day."

"I guess that means I'm lucky to catch you today. Especially just before the start of this rain." Sharon resisted the urge to stick her nose in her elbow to mask the smell.

"You're on your way to Lacey Manor?" the driver asked.

"No, I'm going to the Townsend Farm." Sharon looked ahead into the rain. *A woman!*

The driver nodded.

*Maybe she's selling food on the black market. That would explain why she doesn't want me to know her name.*

"You look like a pilot."

"I am a pilot." *Keep it short and to the point.*

"A woman pilot?"

Sharon nodded.

"What does your Uncle Marmaduke think of that?"

Sharon shrugged. "Only met him once. Besides, I have more important things to worry about instead of what he might or might not think."

They passed through the village of Otley: wet brownstone buildings, slick slate roofs, and bumpy cobblestones.

*Halfway there.*

There was quiet until they reached another village — Burley in Wharfedale. Sharon turned as they passed stone churches. "You don't need to worry. I won't tell anyone about the black market."

The driver looked open-eyed at Sharon. There was a raspy sound, a kind of wheezing laughter.

Sharon checked to see if there was a door handle at the ready in case she needed to jump.

"You think that's why I won't tell ye my name!" The driver slapped the wheel with an open palm. "Think I'm in the black market. Maybe even a highwayman!"

"You have to admit, you're being a bit secretive." Sharon could feel her face glowing with embarrassment.

"No. No, love. I was just waiting to see what kind of Lacey you are! There's two kinds, as far as I can tell. One kind is like that Marmaduke, and the other is like your mother, Leslie. She was salt of the earth. Marmaduke, on the other hand, is more like salt in a wound."

"I've met him. I know what he's like."

"All the women around these parts know what he's like. And none will talk about it." The driver peered though the windshield. "I need to be sure not to miss the road into the Townsend Farm."

She braked, turned, and drove up the lane to Honeysuckle's farm. She stopped near the house.

Sharon opened the door. "Thank you very much for the ride. I would have gotten soaked to the —" She felt a hand on her arm.

"Name's Margaret. I've learned to be a bit cautious in my dealings with the Laceys. I was feeling you out, seeing what sort you are — I owe you a warning, because your mother was always kind to me: be careful in your dealings with that uncle of yours. He can be vicious. He's used to getting what he wants." Margaret released Sharon's arm.

"How do you know?"

"Most of us around these parts know you went to see Walter McGregor, the lawyer. It doesn't take a genius to figure out there's something going on — after all, you are your mother's daughter, and McGregor is a fair and honest man. Lately, I've heard that Marmaduke has been dragging your name through the mud whenever he meets with his posh friends. You would be wise to be careful."

"How do you know about that?"

"Marmaduke has a very loud way about him. And he thinks his servants don't have ears." Margaret released Sharon's arm.

Sharon closed the door, hoisted her bag, and dodged puddles as she ran toward the back door. Before she could knock, the door opened.

"It *is* you!" Honeysuckle waved her inside. "Sean and Linda will be so pleased!"

Sharon let herself be engulfed in Honeysuckle's arms. There was something delicious baking in the oven. *Fresh bread?*

"Was that Margaret who drove you here? Why didn't you call and let us know you were coming?" Honeysuckle released Sharon from her embrace.

"Yes, it was Margaret, and I wanted to surprise you. I hope that's all right." Sharon looked over Honeysuckle's shoulder to see if there was any coffee.

"Come on, sit down at the table. You must be cold. Pour yourself a cuppa. I've got to get the bread out from the oven. Would you like a slice?" Honeysuckle put on oven mitts and opened the oven door.

Sharon grabbed a cup and poured herself a coffee. "I'd love some. It smells just the way my mother's bread smelled. Where are Sean and Linda?"

"Sean's in the barn. He'll be here in a moment. Linda is resting. She just got home from the hospital. Another skin graft. I do hope it's the last. Her spirits are low this time." Honeysuckle set the fresh loaves atop the stove. "How long is your leave?"

"A week." Sharon closed her eyes as she tasted real, fresh-brewed coffee. "Want me to pour you a cup?"

Honeysuckle smiled and nodded. "It's wonderful that you'll have a week with us. Sean will be thrilled. He was very disappointed you weren't allowed home for Christmas." Honeysuckle rubbed the tops of the fresh loaves with butter.

*My mouth is watering.* "We're finally catching up on replacement aircraft. Now the big push is to supply night fighters to take on the Jerry bombers attacking London."

"Well, what do you think of Margaret?" Honeysuckle put the butter down and sat across from Sharon. She lifted her coffee.

"She was feeling me out to see what kind of Lacey I am."

"Sounds like Margaret." Honeysuckle smiled.

"She said my mother did a favour for her?" Sharon watched Honeysuckle's expression.

"Yes, your mother did Margaret a good turn."

"Well, what did she do?"

"When your mother was eighteen, she found out that Margaret was having Marmaduke's child. So Leslie convinced her father to provide a house for Margaret and the baby. Apparently, nothing was ever said to Marmaduke, even though Margaret maintained that she had had no choice in the matter." Honeysuckle blushed.

"You mean that my uncle raped Margaret?"

Honeysuckle nodded.

"Was it a boy or a girl?"

"A boy. He's three years older than you, and the last I heard, he was in a tank in North Africa."

Sharon shook her head. "The more I learn about my family. . ."

"The more interesting it becomes." Honeysuckle raised her eyebrows.

"I wouldn't have put it quite that way." Sharon thought about getting more coffee.

"Just a moment. That bread should have cooled enough for us to have a taste."

Sharon poured more coffee while Honeysuckle cut bread. She set the fresh loaf and some jam on the table.

"So if nothing was ever said about Marmaduke's illegitimate child, why did my mother have to leave the country when she found out about me?"

Honeysuckle carefully spread strawberry jam on her slice of bread. She looked up at Sharon and shrugged. An ageless expression passed between two women who both know the answer to a question, and that answer offers them no comfort. She cut her bread in half and began to eat. Honeysuckle finished chewing. "In a way, your grandmother answered that question."

"What do you mean?"

Honeysuckle picked up her coffee. "Did you know it was your mother who got me drinking coffee? She sent me some for Christmas one year."

"No, I didn't. How did my grandmother answer that question?"

"You remember I told you that Cornelia was going to leave for Canada when she heard your mother was sick?"

Sharon nodded.

"And I explained that the old bastard beat Cornelia so badly, she ended up in hospital?" Honeysuckle asked.

Sharon waited.

"While she was in hospital, they brought in a fellow who had alcohol poisoning. The doctors managed to save him, but it made Cornelia think. You see, she used to stop your grandfather from drinking after he'd had too much. She would hide the bottles; protecting him from himself, it seems. So — I believe it was the day after she got the letter telling her that Leslie had died — she went and bought whiskey. Two cases, if memory serves. At every subsequent evening meal, she kept filling his glass with scotch. When he emptied the glass, she refilled it. She told me a few weeks later that she kept that up every night for a week. Then, I think it was a Friday, she woke up in the morning and found him dead on the dining room floor. He'd choked on his own vomit." Honeysuckle took a sip of coffee, then looked at the bottom of the cup. She stood up. "I think I'll have one more cup. Would you like some more as well?"

Sharon nodded, not knowing what to say.

Honeysuckle refilled their cups. They sat there for a few minutes, drinking coffee, eating fresh bread, and thinking.

"Have you heard from Harry?" Sharon asked.

"He's working in London — 64 Baker Street, in fact. He writes me almost every day."

"What does the address mean?" Sharon asked.

"He's working for what's called the Special Operations Executive, and now so is Michael. He's training agents to go into France, since he can't go back anymore." Honeysuckle put her finger to her lips.

"Why not?" *Just play along. Act like you know less than you do.*

Honeysuckle put her hand on Sharon's. "The Gestapo were onto Michael. Apparently, a Frenchman turned him in to the Germans. He was very nearly arrested. That's why he had to get out of France that night you went to pick him up. Michael's no use on the continent anymore, so they've got him instructing others about what he learned over there."

"They're both safe, then?"

"Safe as anyone else in London with the Blitz going on." Honeysuckle looked at the back door. "Sounds like Sean has finished his chores."

*I wonder how she'll react to our news?*

Boots stamped just outside the kitchen door.

Honeysuckle stood up, looked at Sharon, and lowered her voice. "He's been having nightmares."

Sharon stood.

The door opened. Sean stepped inside; he was bent over after leaving his boots outside. He looked up and saw Honeysuckle. "The bread smells awfully delicious."

"Sean?" Sharon stepped out from behind Honeysuckle.

"Sharon!" Sean rushed across the room, collided with the kitchen table, ricocheted, then hugged her around the waist. He looked up at her. His eyes were underlined with dark smudges from lack of sleep.

He smelled of the barn and wet wool. *He smells wonderful!*

"There's fresh bread on the table. Hang your jacket up, wash up, and sit down with us." There was satisfaction and contentment behind Honeysuckle's tone.

A minute later, Sean was sitting next to Sharon, slathering jam onto his bread, and wearing a milk moustache. "What have you flown lately?" He looked at his sister.

"There was a remarkable twin-engined aircraft I got to fly the other day. Unfortunately, there's not much more I can say about it, other than it's very fast." Sharon put her hand on Sean's back.

"As fast as a Spitfire?"

"Faster."

"You must be joking!"

"Not a bit of it." Sharon looked at Honeysuckle, who was holding her coffee cup and smiling from behind it. "Before I forget." Sharon picked up her duffel bag. "I happened upon a generous supply of chocolate." She reached inside, pulled out a bar, and handed it to Sean.

Sean's smile was nothing compared to the look of rapture on his face after his first bite of the chocolate.

# CHAPTER 30

**"Come on. I have an appointment in Ilkley,** and you need to get out for a bit." Sharon and Linda were bundled up and sitting outside in the garden. Linda had her legs up and sat sideways in her chair. She rolled a cigarette between the thumb and forefinger of her left hand and drank tea with her right. Her red hair was in desperate need of a wash, cut, and brush. Her cheeks were hollow and her eyes vacant.

"Do you have to be so damned cheerful and ambitious?" Linda tried to smile and almost succeeded.

*You look like hell.* "I'd like to bring Sean, and there will be a surprise for you, too."

"I look like hell."

"Look, you can stay at home playing the melancholy heroine, or you can get off your sore backside and come with us." Sharon waited for an angry response. *Come on, for Christ's sake, Linda, fight back!* "We've made an appointment for you at the hairdressers. I need to see the solicitor. After that, we can get some fish and chips."

"All food tastes like paste these days." Linda looked away from her friend and stared at something in the middle distance.

"What happened at the hospital?"

"More skin grafts."

"I know that. What else?" Sharon leaned forward to be in Linda's field of vision.

"The day I arrived, they brought in a sergeant pilot. He was nineteen or twenty. His fingers, ears, and nose were burned off. He was screaming in agony. Some idiot put tannic acid on the burns before he was brought to the hospital. The staff tried a variety of different treatments, but infection set in. It took him four days to die." Linda looked at her friend. "And here I am, feeling maudlin because I've had another set of skin grafts. Thinking that no one is going to want to dance with me because my legs look like this." She lifted the blanket to reveal a nightmare of mottled scar tissue reaching from just below the knees to just above the ankles. "He dies and I live. How does that make the least bit of sense? And why do I feel so guilty for having survived? I should be happy to be alive."

*What do I say to her?*

"You don't have to say anything. Everyone else walks around here on eggshells. I wish someone would scream or yell or cry. You know that I don't even feel like crying? I just feel exhausted all the time." Linda shook her head.

"Shit!"

Linda was startled. A shiver ran through her.

A flock of birds bounced into the sky, frightened from their perches in a leafless tree.

"When I said I wished someone would scream, I was joking," Linda said.

"Come into town with Sean and me," Sharon said. "Please."

Linda frowned. "You're not going to give up on this, are you?"

"No, I'm not."

Linda pushed herself up out of her chair. "Well, let's get going, then."

It took Sean five minutes to get ready. Sharon took ten, and Linda took ninety.

Linda drove from the back seat as Sharon steered the black four-door Morris with its reluctant gears and touchy clutch.

"Turn here!" Linda said.

"Which way?" Sharon asked.

"To the right, of course!" Linda said.

"You've lived here all of your life. I haven't."

"Your mother was born here. It should be an instinctive inheritance courtesy of your blue blood."

Sean began to laugh.

By the time they stopped in front of the hairdresser's shop, all three were laughing.

"Pick you up in an hour?" Sharon asked.

Linda opened the suicide door and followed her legs out. "That should do it. If not, I'll wait here for you." She shut the door and waved as they drove away.

Sean said, "That's the first time she's smiled since she got back from the hospital, just before Christmas."

Sharon drove to the office of Walter McGregor and parked out front.

"Do you want me to wait here?" Sean asked.

"No, come on in with me. This concerns you as well. Besides, I'd like to spend as much time as possible with you." Sharon opened her door and got out.

"How did you sleep last night?"

"All right, I suppose."

"I had a wonderful sleep. No nightmare for a change." Sharon walked toward the door to McGregor's office.

"You have nightmares, too?"

Sharon heard the tension in his voice. "Yes. Mostly I find myself trapped in the cockpit. There are flames inside and out. Sometimes I wake up and I believe I can still smell burning flesh in the room." She reached for the office door handle and waited.

Sean said, "I'm trapped underground and I'm choking on dust."

"Sounds horrible."

Sean nodded and turned his worried eyes on her. "I wake up choking and gasping for breath sometimes."

"I'm glad I live alone, because I think I wake up screaming."

"I wake Honeysuckle up." Sean looked at Sharon and cocked his head to one side. "I thought it was just me."

"No." Sharon hugged him around the shoulders. "Both of us have been through quite a bit in this war. But we're definitely not the only ones having nightmares."

Sean leaned into her. "I'm glad you came."

"So am I."

She opened the door. "Come on, let's see what Mr. McGregor has to say."

The secretary's desk was empty, and the door to Walter McGregor's office was open. He stood up from behind his desk when he heard the door close behind Sharon. "There you are. Do come in."

Sharon gently guided Sean in ahead of her as Walter cleared papers, files, and newspapers from two chairs.

"Sit down, please." McGregor looked at Sharon and her brother.

*He looks different. He's cut his hair, but there is something else as well.* "You look well." She sat down next to Sean.

"Thank you. I, er, *we've* received word from both our sons. The one has been sent to train other pilots, and the other has a leave coming up. It will be good to see him again. Safe from the convoys and the U-boat wolf packs for at least a little while." Walter searched his desk, thumbing through one pile. "Ah, here it is."

Sharon leaned forward.

He opened the file and handed her a letter. "There has been progress in your case. Your grandmother wrote a letter. She must have heard about your claim from Marmaduke. Can't say he'll be pleased by what she's written." He handed her the letter.

DEAR MR. MCGREGOR,

FIRST OF ALL, LET ME PUT YOUR MIND AT EASE. AS LONG AS I AM ALIVE, YOU WILL CONTINUE TO BE THE LACEY FAMILY'S SOLICITOR. MY SON CAN THREATEN ALL HE WANTS, BUT I WILL HAVE THE FINAL SAY IN THE MATTER.

SECONDLY, I AM CERTAIN THAT SHARON LACEY IS, IN FACT, THE DAUGHTER OF LESLIE LACEY. ANYONE WHO KNEW MY DAUGHTER LESLIE CAN SEE THAT THE RESEMBLANCE BETWEEN THE TWO IS REMARKABLE. BESIDES, IN HER LETTERS HOME, LESLIE OFTEN SPOKE OF SHARON, HER INTERESTS, AND HER STRENGTH OF CHARACTER.

AS MY RIGHTFUL GRANDDAUGHTER, SHARON LACEY IS ENTITLED TO HER MOTHER'S SHARE OF THE LACEY INHERITANCE.

THIS LETTER, THEREFORE, IS MY RECOGNITION OF SHARON LACEY
AS A LEGAL DESCENDANT OF MINE. IT IS ALSO A LETTER OF INTENT
THAT I WILL SIT DOWN WITH YOU, MR. MCGREGOR, AND FORMALIZE
A NEW WILL AT YOUR EARLIEST POSSIBLE CONVENIENCE.

YOURS TRULY,
MRS. CORNELIA LACEY

Sharon handed the letter back to Walter. "Thank you." *Why do I feel like crying?*

"Lady Lacey came in last week to sign a new will. You are recognized in that will as the daughter of Leslie and a beneficiary of the estate." Walter's oak chair groaned as he leaned back. "As far as the rest of the will is concerned, it is up to your grandmother whether or not she wishes to divulge more information about the details of your inheritance."

Sean tugged his sister's blouse. "Why are you crying?"

"I don't know."

McGregor handed her his handkerchief. "I am also obliged to offer a warning about your Uncle Marmaduke."

Sharon wiped her eyes and nose. She balled the handkerchief in her hand. "Yes?"

"He is a vengeful man who is unfamiliar with the taste of defeat, especially at the hands of a woman. He will choose another weapon. Character assassination will be his most likely course of action."

Sharon remembered the ATA pilots at White Waltham talking behind their hands. "What have I gotten you into?"

Walter smiled. "Actually, I've begun to feel alive again. I have my own little war to fight while my sons are off fighting the bigger battles. And I have you to thank for this newfound joie de vivre."

o **"So what is the surprise you've been talking about?"** Linda sat in the backseat with freshly shampooed and cut hair. They caught the scent of strawberries.

Sharon looked at her wristwatch. "First, some lunch, then the surprise." She drove along the main street until she came to Guy Fawkes Pub and parked across the street.

"And you thought I was lying when I said it runs through that blue blood of yours. Case in point. Your kind always knows where to find a pub. And this is one of the best in West Yorkshire," Linda said.

Sharon turned off the engine and looked in the rear-view mirror. She couldn't tell if Linda was smiling or frowning. She got out of the Morris and waited at the front door of the Fawkes.

Sean held the door for them as they went inside. They were greeted with the scents of pipe smoke, hops, and fermentation.

They sat by one of two windows and ordered food.

"So what is this surprise?" Linda asked.

"You'll have to wait," Sharon said.

"Is it more chocolate?" Sean asked.

"A promotion celebration?" Linda asked.

Sharon blushed.

"Christ, I'm right. You got a promotion?" Linda sat back and rolled her eyes. Then she looked at Sharon. "I've become such a miserable Angus. You get a promotion, and all I feel is jealousy."

"She keeps calling herself a cow," Sean said.

Sharon smiled. "Well, I'd say you're more like a Charolais."

"If you want my opinion, you're more like a Limousin." Michael stood next to Sean.

"Michael!" Linda stood up and hugged her brother.

"It *is* you!" Sean looked sideways at his sister, gauging her reaction.

"One advantage to living in Yorkshire is that we certainly know a great deal about cows." Michael held Linda away from him. "You've cut your hair."

"How would you know? You haven't seen me in months! Still, this is a wonderful surprise." Linda looked at Sharon. "This is your surprise for me?"

Sharon nodded.

Michael put his hand on Sharon's shoulder.

Sean looked from Michael to Sharon.

"What have the two of you been up to?" Linda asked.

Michael pulled up a chair and sat next to Sean. "A trip to the theatre in London, a few dinners. Mostly, we went for walks, because it has been the only option with the time available."

"White Waltham is close to London. And the train goes right through Maidenhead. Just down the road, really," Sharon said.

"Why didn't you tell us?" Linda looked at Sean.

Sharon and Michael looked at one another.

"We wanted to be sure, is all," Michael said.

"Before we told you," Sharon said.

"What about Mother?" Linda asked.

"She knows," Michael said.

"How?" Linda asked.

"Father told her," Michael said.

"Why does he have to know every damned thing that goes on?" Linda began to laugh.

"What's so hilarious?" Sean asked.

"Sharon comes all this way looking to meet her father, and she ends up with a whole family!" Linda pointed at her friend. "Just promise me one thing: don't name your first-born Marmaduke." Linda laughed some more.

Sharon looked around the table as Michael looked at Sean. Her brother sat back in his chair, then laughter jumped out of him.

Michael leaned over and said to Sharon, "I'm afraid I've only got four days. Will it be enough?"

She leaned into him. "It will do for now."

# ACKNOWLEDGEMENTS

Bruce, for caring for us all these years thank you.

MaryAnne, thanks for the invaluable advice and for reading the first drafts.

Again, thanks to Wayne Gunn.

Thanks to the Canadian Aviation Museum in Ottawa, the Alberta Aviation Museum in Edmonton, the Aero Space Museum of Calgary, and the Military Museums in Calgary.

Mary, Alex K., Ernie, and Sebi thanks for the suggestions and feedback. Doug, Lou, Paul, Jenna, Natalie, Andrew, Matt, Michael, Cathy, and Tiiu, thank you.

Thanks to creative writers at Nickle, Bowness, Lord Beaverbrook, Alternative, Forest Lawn, and Queen Elizabeth.

Sharon, Karma, Ben, Luke, Indiana, and Ella. Well?

# SOURCES

## DVD

*Foyle's War*, Acorn Media
*Piece of Cake*, based on Derek Robinson's best-selling novel, Granada
    International
*Island at War*, Acorn Media, Granada International

## PRINT

*Reach for the Sky*, Paul Brickhill
*Ginger Lacey Fighter Pilot*, Richard Townshend Bickers
*Spitfire Summer: When Britain Stood Alone*, Malcolm Brown
*The Big Show (Le Grand Cirque)*, Pierre Clostermann
*The Narrow Margin*, Derek Wood with Derek Dempster
*James Herriot's Yorkshire*, James Herriot and photographer Derry Brabbs
*Duel of Eagles*, Peter Townsend
*Mosquito*, text by Bill Sweetman / illustrations by Rikyu Watanabe
*Newnes' Motorists' Touring Maps and Gazetteer*, Complete Section Maps of
    the British Isles, George Newnes, Limited, Tower House, Southampton
    Street, Strand, W.C. 2
*Aeroplane Monthly Magazine*, May, June, July 1990

**GARRY RYAN** taught for a little over thirty years in Calgary Public Schools. In 2004, he published his first Detective Lane novel, *Queen's Park*. The second, *The Lucky Elephant Restaurant*, won a 2007 Lambda Literary Award. He has since published three more titles in the series: *A Hummingbird Dance*, *Smoked*, and *Malabarista*. In 2009, Ryan was awarded Calgary's Freedom of Expression Award. *Blackbirds* is his sixth novel with NeWest, and the first in a new series.